KEEPING UP WITH PJ

Stories from the 1950s Rural South.

DON MICHAEL FLOURNOY

STEPHEN F. AUSTIN STATE UNIVERSITY PRESS
2019

IN THE YEAR 1950, PJ Purdee is a 14-year-old boy living in an agricultural community in the southern region of the United States. PJ has a restless disposition, and a curiosity and intelligence beyond his years. As a barefoot runner, he is likely to show up almost anywhere along the sandy roads that reach out from the cotton farms of the prairie into the impenetrable thicket grown up in the miles of Cutover where a virgin longleaf pine forest once stood.

PJ's father was killed in World War II. His mother now commutes six days a week to work at a poultry processing plant at the county seat some 30 miles from home. When not in school, PJ and his older brother Roy often find themselves free to do whatever they like.

These two boys spend most of their time on Sandy Prairie, a crossroad community that boasts a grocery and feed store, a cotton gin, a two-teacher school and a church. Local businessman Cyrus Sapp owns the gin, the store and several farms in the vicinity, as well as the tenant house rented by PJ's mother Belle. Mr. Sapp has taken a liking to PJ and counts on him as a ready helper. PJ, who is white, crosses easily into the local African American community, especially with the Nettie Johnson family, a close relationship he has had since the day he was born.

As this story picks up in early summer 1950, PJ is finally old enough to do a man's work, not only among the truck farms and cotton fields of the Prairie, but also in the cotton gin. While the boy gains acceptance and appreciation almost everywhere, and is feeling the exhilaration of being treated for the first time like an adult, his mother Belle is in a far different place in her life. She is on the verge of making a decision that will change her sons' future forever.

The voice of this fictional narrative, as well as pencil drawings dating back to the 1950s, is that of Dr. Peyton Jackson Purdee whose children and grandchildren convinced him to write down some of the tales he had told over the years about growing up in Theodosa County.

TABLE OF CONTENTS

THE BIG OLD PECKERWOOD

PJ heard the limb of the chinaberry tree crack beneath him. It made a sound like a .22 rifle shot. He was grabbing at leaves as he fell.

He never hit the ground because he was awake and sitting up in his bed. It was daylight. Roy was gone from his side of the bed. The guinea hens were all stirred up and making racket outside.

He had to step over clothes that had been thrown around on the floor. Roy never picked up anything. It made PJ mad, his brother leaving things strewn about. PJ picked up a towel, a sweaty t-shirt and some socks and put them with the other dirty clothes in the corner of their bedroom, but he couldn't find his pants.

From the dresser, he took a clean pair of overalls and put them on without a shirt or shoes. He went out the screen door onto the porch.

Roy was standing out in the lane, also barefooted. He had the rifle in one hand. He was looking out toward the Dominey pasture. "I got him," he said as if he knew his brother would be standing there watching him. PJ could see that Roy had on his pants, his good ones, the ones he had hung on the door when they got home from the picture show last night.

"What you shootin' at?" PJ asked.

"There. Over there." Roy pointed to the big sycamore that used to be in the yard of the Dominey house, when the Dominey house was still there. "He got up and flew off. But I hit him all right."

"Hit what?"

"Peckerwood. Biggest one you ever saw."

"What you shootin' at him for?"

"Didn't you hear him? All that racket. Sounded like a tommy gun."

"Naw," PJ said aloud to let Roy know how irritated he was. "I was asleep."

"Nobody can sleep with all that at-tat-tat going on." Roy seemed to like hearing his own imitation of the big woodpecker, for he called out several "at-tat-tats" in a row as he walked over and laid the barrel of the gun—that belonged to the two of them —up on a fence post to make it more steady.

He took a quick look down the sight. "What'll you give me if I can hit him from here?"

"I can't even see where he's at."

"On that limb toward the creek. High up there."

The Dominey tree was dead in the top, struck by lightning in an electrical storm. Roy and PJ had heard it happen. They had climbed the fence to see the fresh scar that ran down its trunk. They had counted seven crows lying dead on the ground.

PJ crossed the road and came up to the fence where his brother had taken up position. "Yeah, I can see him now."

"What'll you give me?"

"I'm not giving you anything because I don't think you ought to be shootin' those kinds of birds."

Roy was like that. He would kill things for no reason at all. "It's just an old woodpecker," he said.

"Leave it alone. It's not bothering you."

"It woke me up. . . Christ A'mighty, it ain't good for nothin'."

"Well you'd just be wastin' bullets. You won't hit it. You can't hardly see it from here."

Roy flipped the empty shell out of the chamber and put in a .22-long. He sighted down the barrel and fired. The bird was high up in the tree. When the bullet hit there was no sound, just a ball of feathers exploding into the air.

Suddenly there were wings opened, catching the wind. The wings carried the bird gently sailing across the field, touching lightly the tops of the goat weeds. It landed abruptly in a heap not ten feet from where Roy and his brother stood.

"Wow! What you say to that?"

"Lucky."

"Lucky, my foot. That's good aim," Roy said. "And I didn't

even have to go over there and get it."

"You wouldn't have gone got it anyway."

"I would've. I been wantin' to see what one of these big peckers looks like up close."

Roy handed PJ the rifle. He lifted the barbed wire and climbed through the fence. He went over and walked around the dead bird, sizing it up. The woodpecker was stretched out on the ground like a navy plane that had come in for a crash landing.

Roy picked it up by one wing. Its wingspread was almost as wide as he could reach. It had the kind of feathers the Alabama Coushattas made necklaces out of, long black feathers with white along the bottom.

"Look at the bill on that thing," Roy said, admiring it.

The bird's head hung lifeless across its body, its ivory beak locked open as if it had died screaming.

Holding onto the one wing, Roy whirled all the way around to get his momentum and threw the bird over the fence as high into the air as he could. It came down with a thud in the soft dirt of the lane. "I thought we might get it to sail like it did before," Roy said climbing back through the fence.

He picked up the carcass, shook the sand out and started toward the house. One wing was dragging the ground.

"What're you going to do with it now?"

"I'm going to tack it up out here on the side of the woodshed."

"What for?"

"So people can look at it from the road. It's a pretty thing to see."

Roy dropped the carcass over by the shed. He then went and got a hammer and some nails off the back porch. "Hold it up for me," he instructed PJ, "so I can nail it up."

PJ reached down and picked the bird up by its two wings and, in doing so, he was able to get a good look it. He had never seen one of these ivorybill woodpeckers up-close. Only the top of its head, a brilliant pyramid of red, seemed untouched, not yet drained of all life.

He couldn't help but shake his head in disbelief that Roy would kill such a beautiful creature as this. "This is a shame," he said to no one but himself. He didn't want to but went ahead anyway and held the bird up against the shed.

Roy took the hammer and nailed through the wing on one side and then on the other. When he saw that the head had flopped over, he went into the shed and found a piece of electrical wire that he could wrap around the neck. Then he positioned a nail higher up and hammered it in place so the head was looking up.

Roy had just stepped back to admire his work when their mother Belle called through the screen of her bedroom. "Would you boys stop that. . . ! How am I going to sleep with you doing all that hammering?"

PJ apologized. "Sorry, Mom. We forgot you were sleeping,"

"We got us a peckerwood," Roy said in quick reply.

"A what?"

"One of those big old woodpeckers. You know. You ought to come out and see him."

"This is my only day to sleep in. . . . Why don't you boys find somewhere else to make all that racket."

HOEING WITH GUY STOOKEY

"You ain't going to ask him nothing like that."

"You want to bet? What you bet me I'll do it?"

"Yeah, you'd do it all right. You'd do most anything. But that don't mean you ought to." It bothered PJ that his brother would come right out and ask somebody something like that.

Roy dropped his hoe and picked up a rock from the sand at his feet. "I'll git his attention." The rock was already hot from the morning sun. He bounced it in his hand to show PJ he was going to throw it.

PJ knew it wasn't any use trying to stop him. Once Roy made up his mind to do something, he was more likely to go ahead and do it if you said he oughtn't than if you said he should.

Roy threw the rock. It landed a few yards shy of where Guy Stookey was chopping cotton ahead of them. The rock kicked up a little puff of dust among the dry cotton rows.

Stookey didn't notice. Roy picked up another rock. "Why don't you just call to him? You goin to hit him." PJ cautioned, knowing what he said wouldn't make any difference to Roy.

The second rock landed closer. Stookey raised up from his hoeing on the cotton row ahead of them and looked around. The long rows stretched as far in front of him as behind him. The man seemed fragile as a dried cornstalk in the waves of rising heat.

"Guy," Roy shouted. "How about a catch-up?"

Stookey turned, waved and started working back toward the two boys. Roy nodded his head sharply with satisfaction, and smiled at PJ as if to prove he could talk a squirrel down out of a tree.

"You going to make him mad," PJ said.

"No, I ain't."

11

PJ and his brother set to work in earnest. The hoeing wasn't hard, except for the low places where the Bermuda grass had taken hold. A good working rhythm to thin the young cotton plants in the row and remove the competing weeds and grass came easy in the dry sandy soil.

PJ's bare feet sought out the soft earth recently broken in the adjacent row by Stookey's strong even strokes. He didn't mind the work, so long as there was somebody to work with.

PJ was thinking, they aren't going to be leaving me behind this year. He'd vowed that to himself even before school was out. He was a lot bigger now, now that he was 14 years old.

"Grown two inches this year," his mother Belle had said. PJ had gone up to the brick house with his mother to see their landlord Cyrus Sapp about putting off paying the rent.

Their old car had to have new tires. Belle joked with Mr. Sapp. "He's got so big I can't whup him no more."

Mr. Sapp laughed at that and said, "I wouldn't think you'd ever have to whip PJ."

Cyrus Sapp owned both the store and the cotton gin on the Prairie. Five different tenant farm families lived on Sapp properties growing cotton and peanuts, mostly working the land on halves. Belle and her two boys lived in one of the Sapp houses, but just paid straight rent.

"No, I never have," she admitted.

"Well, he's a fine young man. You should be proud."

Back in the cotton field, PJ was thinking he would have been working up there alongside Guy right now if it hadn't been for Roy. He knew he shouldn't let Roy distract him, but he did.

Roy could work as hard and for as long as anybody when he wanted to. Roy was 16, two years, two months and two days older than PJ, but he had asthma – or used to – so bad didn't anybody expect much out of him anymore. There had been times Roy couldn't get his breath and it made people think he was about to die.

Ahead, they could hear Guy Stookey's hoe bite into the parched ground. PJ glanced up and saw that Guy was hoeing two rows at once. He admired that. Everybody said what a good worker Guy Stookey was.

PJ tried matching Stookey's steady pace, taking a stroke every time Stookey did, listening for their hoes to fall in time. It pleased him he was able to do it.

"There y'are," Stookey said, giving his last few licks to Roy's row. He straightened and paused for a moment as if wondering why the boys called to him. "Y'all caught up with me now."

"I don't see how you get so far ahead, Guy," PJ said.

He looked at PJ and kidded him a little bit. "PJ, the secret to success in hoeing is to move your hoe every once in a while."

PJ took that to mean that Guy thought he and Roy were spending too much time talking and not enough time working. "Heavy grass back there," PJ complained. It wasn't so, and Guy would know that, but he'd said it before he thought. He didn't like for Guy Stookey to have the idea he was lazy.

Roy took the offense. "PJ, he's just twice as big as us, that's all."

Guy looked puzzled. "When you're twice as big you got to stoop twice as far. When I was your age I was a better hoe hand than I am now."

Roy replied, "When you're tall you git all the breeze."

"That could be. But it ain't no advantage on a day like today. Ain't been a bit of breeze." Stookey dug the blade of his hoe into the ground and tamped on it with his foot so that the hoe stood upright on its own. He took off his sweaty bill cap, hung it on the handle, and sat down right on the hot ground. "Got enough dirt collected here to make another terrace row," he said as he emptied his shoes of sand.

The two boys promptly sat down as well. PJ took off his old train conductor's cap and Roy removed the wide-brim straw hat that Belle made him wear out in the sun. They didn't need to take off their shoes. They didn't wear any, ever, summer or winter.

People said Guy Stookey was so long and skinny you could use him as a rope. It'd have to be a lariat rope, PJ had concluded. The lariat rope was an unbreakable rope they used in handling steers at the livestock auction. Artis Pixley was the one who had said that. "That fellow's muscles are wove so tight you could bend him double and he still wouldn't break."

PJ had watched Guy digging the new cistern at school, and he had seen the way he could roll those big 500-pound bales of cotton around at the gin.

Skinny guys'll fool you, PJ thought. You can bend a hickory sapling or a persimmon sprout all the way to the ground, but they'll whip right back up. That's what being tough means. PJ knew that was the kind of man he wanted to grow up to be.

Watching Guy take off his shoes, PJ marveled that feet of such size would be attached to such thin ankles. His wrists were the same way. Against them his hands seemed oversized; his long mechanic's fingers, thick and scarred, seemed too long.

PJ decided there was a lot he didn't know about Guy Stookey, and he would like to know him better.

There were the tales people were always telling on Guy (never to his face) but you didn't know how much of that to believe. He had heard the story about Guy sailing off the Shawnee bridge into a dry creek bed going 80 miles an hour. They say he just put his old souped-up Chevrolet in low gear and spun up out of there with three of four tires blowed out. Of course, that was a long time ago.

PJ had been there when Guy brought his coon dog with him to church and the dog sang right along with everybody else. Mr. Beeman, manager of the store, said he had watched Guy drink a 16-ounce RC Cola without taking a breath. And he wasn't even showing off.

Even in the suffering heat of the summer, Guy Stookey's heavy khaki shirt was buttoned at the sleeves, and his collar was turned up around his neck to protect his skin from the burning sun. Under his bill cap, his sandy hair was pale and damp, while on his face and on the sides and back of his head the hair bristled and his flesh was raw red as if it had been sand papered.

On the back of Guy's neck was a knot the size of a baseball that he protected from the sun with a faded bandana.

Doc Jackson called it a "wen." It was burned dry and crusty around its edges and PJ thought it looked inflamed.

Wherever the sun struck Guy Stookey his skin seemed to peel away in layers. Sweat had soaked through his shirt. The outline of perspiration along Guy's shoulders and backbone looked like the jagged remains of a T-bone steak, and the smell from his underarms seared the air as it all rose up with the heat.

"Your titties are leaking there, Guy," Roy said, pointing to the large greasy spots spread out from the two front pockets of Guy's shirt.

"Yeah?" Stookey looked down. "Yeah, looks like it, don't it?" he said grinning. He reached into his shirt pocket and pulled out an enormous biscuit that he extended in Roy's direction and then to PJ. "You want a bite?"

"No. Don't believe so. Thanks anyway." PJ knew it was what Grace Stookey always fixed Guy for his midday meal: two big lard biscuits with a hard-fried egg and a chunk of bacon in between. He was known to start eating on those biscuits halfway through the morning, rolling them around in his mouth like a chew of tobacco. When everybody else was calling it quits for dinner, Stookey just came in to get his drink of water but went right on back to work. If somebody asked, he just said, "Thank yah. I done ate."

Who's making those biscuits now, PJ wondered, if what they say about Grace is true?

Stookey took a big bite of the egg and bacon sandwich. He had a couple of teeth missing so he had to bite to one side. Squatting there in front of him, Roy seemed to be studying him. Roy was about to come out with something, PJ could tell. His brother never let anything rest.

Roy asked. "Did you salt them eggs before you put 'em in that pocket there, Guy?"

"Yeah, I salts 'em. Peppers 'em."

"Well, I see now why you don't need to salt 'em any more, Guy. Your sweat done soaked right through that shirt into that biscuit. So, you shouldn't need no more salt."

Guy seemed appreciative of the idea. "How about that. . . Roy you are really something. I never thought of that before." He then took another bite of the biscuit and stuffed what was left of it back into his shirt pocket, wiping his hands on the front of his shirt. "Well, boys, we better git back at it."

He put one hand on the ground and pulled himself upright with the other, using his hoe for support. "Your Granny'll be looking out her kitchen window wondering how much of this sitting around she's goin' to have to pay for."

PJ was thinking, I'm going to have to do a lot of growing, if I'm ever going to be that tall.

They had just put their hoes on their shoulders and were walking up the rows to where Guy had begun helping to bring them up to where he was when Roy started poking fun at him again. "Guy, I been meaning to ask you a question."

PJ looked quickly up to see how Stookey would react. Roy's bound to get us both in trouble, he told himself. He didn't know why Roy had to pick at things.

"Yeah?"

"I heard that you could lift a hundred pound sack of cottonseed meal with your teeth."

"Where'd you hear that?"

"I heard it."

"I don't do that no more. When I was ten years younger I had ten years less sense."

"Could you do that?"

"Yeah, I done it."

"That why you got them teeth missing?"

"Naw, there's nothing to that." He opened his mouth so the boys could see. He still had a biscuit ball in his jaw. "Lost these teeth working a team in the woods. Limb flew back and hit me in the face."

PJ cringed. "Knock 'em clean out?" he asked.

"Pretty near."

Roy was playing at pole vaulting, running forward, taking little leaps on his hoe. "I got another question for you."

Stookey didn't say anything.

"How come you got that knot on your neck?"

"It's jest a wen."

"Does it hurt?"

"Naw, it don't hurt." Stookey pulled down the faded bandana covering the dry red skin that stretched over the growth. He poked at it with his finger, and then put his finger up to his nose. "It sometimes smells somethin' awful... but it don't hurt."

Roy wasn't being entirely out of hand with his questions but PJ had reason to be suspicious. Roy did not know when to stop.

"Then it's not true what I heard?"

Stookey paused and turned. Roy was so close to him the sun wasn't in Roy's face when he looked up. Stookey seemed a little agitated.

"I heard," Roy said, moving away, "you swallowed a goose egg."

"No, I didn't swallow no egg."

There was a pause and Guy was about to walk on when Roy added, "I heard something else."

"No, I didn't swallow no hickernuts neither."

"Well, that's what I heard. . . one of your nuts got out of place."

Stookey got redder in the face. "What's that you said, boy?"

Roy backed away like he thought Stookey might go after him. It seemed clear to PJ that Roy was trying to provoke him. He was even enjoying it. That sort of thing made PJ feel embarrassed and very uneasy.

"I heard that Stookey's got more balls than anybody. He's got one in his neck."

The line of Stookey's mouth hardened. The muscles in his jaw quivered. "If you're gonna be a smart aleck, Roy Purdee, I won't be catching you up again."

Pointing to the row beside him, Guy said, "Come on, PJ, you and me'll just work off and leave Mr. Sassypants by hisself. When your Granny looks out here and sees him dragging along behind, she won't be for paying him nothing."

Positioning himself a hoe-handle distance from the cotton row, Stookey spat on his hands, leaned forward and started working at an ever-faster pace.

Roy persisted from behind. "What is the story on that thing?" Stookey did not look up. His face glowed red. The wen on his neck bobbed loosely under the bandana as he worked.

PJ felt relieved. At least Guy wasn't mad at him. He sure would have been if Roy had gone into that business about Stookey's wife.

PJ was even a little flattered. He was beginning to think that Guy Stookey was wanting him to be up with him. He remembered the way it was last year at the gin. The cotton wagons were lined up before the scales. The suction feeder was emptying a wagon every 30 minutes. Stookey was falling behind at the press, and Mr. Sapp sent PJ up to see if he could use a hand. In no time at all, Stookey had PJ tying out 500-pound bales of lint cotton like he was a full-grown man, and he wasn't but 13 years old then.

Because Guy hoed half of PJ's row as well as his own, Roy was soon left behind. PJ could tell by the sound of his hoe hitting the ground that Roy was working hard to stay up. He felt an impulse to put in a lick or two every now and then on Roy's row, just to let him know he was thinking of him, but he was afraid Guy wouldn't like it. Roy's my brother, he told himself, but if I got to choose, I'd just as soon stay up here with Guy.

PJ worked quietly. It was all he could do to keep the pace that Guy had set. When he fell behind, he would look up and see Guy carrying both their rows until they were even again. It was as if Guy wanted to keep PJ close to him.

That was the way PJ had felt when they were working the press. Wasn't any use trying to talk inside the gin. Cotton gins made way too much noise for anybody to hear, and nearly everybody kept their ears stuffed with cotton anyway and just used hand signals. He quickly found out, if you paid attention, you could see what needed to be done. And Guy was right there, watching him and giving him the right sign at the right time.

It was like we were all one person with eagle eyes and many arms and legs moving in different directions to turn out a finished bale of lint cotton every 30 minutes, bale after bale until the last wagon had gone home for the night. That's what a cotton gin is, PJ said to himself.

When Guy Stookey finally said something, it startled PJ. "Doc Jackson, he tole me that it wasn't nothin' to worry about."

PJ didn't know if he was expected to say something or not. He was struggling to keep up so he didn't say anything.

"To be honest with you, PJ, my wife Grace, she thinks this here wen is disgusting. She calls it putrid and says it smells like something dead."

Guy's head never came up and his hoe kept seeking out the little sprigs of grass and places where the cotton plants needed thinning, never breaking rhythm.

"It don't smell that bad. . . just some fatty stuff. The doctor could'a cut it off if I'd a wanted him to. I just didn't want to be laid up and lose the time at work."

Then it must not be true, PJ thought, that the reason Guy and Grace Stookey don't have any children is that one of Guy's cods is up around his neck.

Guy must have read his mind, because he then said, "Why is it people talk about what's none of their business, tell me that?"

The question bothered PJ. It didn't seem right he should have to answer for other people. "Don't nobody talk," PJ lied.

"Artis Pixley thought just what Roy thought. Grace's the one who told me that. If people wasn't talkin' about it, where would Roy a'picked that up, tell me that? . . . It's common sense. Anybody would a'known a wen on your neck don't have nothin' to do with nothin'."

On the boys' side of the outhouse at school somebody had gone to a lot of trouble to write out a little ditty. It went like this:

> If Guy's got the big one
> and we all think he's the best
> Whys Grace havin' so much fun
> puttin' everybody else to the test?

For as long as he could remember, PJ'd heard talk about Grace, and everybody knew about the time Grace was keeping house for the Beemans and got fired because Mrs. Beeman, who was teaching school in town, found out her husband was going home in the middle of the day.

PJ had wondered how much of that was true. He thought an

awful lot of Mr. Beeman, the manager of the Crossroads store, and that just didn't seem right.

They hoed in silence for a few minutes. "PJ? Did you know Grace left me?"

PJ was stunned. He had heard it. It was what Roy wanted to know about. But PJ didn't feel right talking about it. Reluctantly, he admitted, "Yeah, I did hear that."

"What have you heard?"

The sand had grown hot. PJ's bare feet found little shade under the leaves of the young cotton stalks. He had to watch that he wasn't stepping on the plants. The sun baked down on the back of his neck, and the unnaturally fast pace wore at him. "Nothin', really."

"When I come home Tuesday ev'nin there wasn't no supper on. PJ, that's the first time that happened in ten years. Ten years."

Stookey's hoe rose higher and higher with each stroke, cutting through the ground in neat, evenly spaced intervals. He was working PJ's row almost as much as his own. "You ain't heard where she went to, did you PJ?"

"I heard she was gone. I haven't heard anybody say where she was."

"She take up with somebody?"

"I don't know, Guy. I really don't know."

"It's that Artis Pixley, ain't it?" There was anger and hurt in his voice. "I saw he'd come back. Now he's gone again, ain't he?"

"Hey," Roy called from behind. "How about a help-up?"

PJ felt bad about leaving Roy back there by himself. "You think we ought to help him up?" he asked Stookey.

"Naw, let him alone." Stookey seemed put out with Roy and all his type.

PJ looked to see how far it was to the end of the row. He called back to Roy, cupping his hand alongside his mouth, "When we git out . . . "

"Come on, fellows," Roy pleaded, making a big display of his hoeing to show he was working.

Guy was still talking: "I figured she was over to Claire Ruth's. Claire Ruth said she hadn't seen her since church on Sunday.

She wasn't at Bertha Pixley's neither . . . . They lying. They know where she's at. They just won't tell me." Stookey's face was flushed and his chest was heaving. "I don't know but what she might be hurt or something."

My God, don't cry, PJ thought. The only time he had ever seen a grown man cry was when Beryl Forkner's babies got burned up in the fire that destroyed their house while he had gone fishing to the River. He hoped Guy wouldn't cry.

Stookey never looked up. He just kept on working. "I wanted children, PJ. I did. I'd like to have me a boy. Maybe one that'd grow up to be like you."

That was hard for PJ to imagine. All he could think of was the goose-egg-size wen that he and Guy would share in common and that the two of them would stride out to the field every morning with egg and bacon biscuits in their shirt pockets. But then, it did seem something was wrong if Guy wanted kids and didn't have any.

"I might a'thought it was a problem with me if I was the only'est one she took to. Wouldn't you figure it that way?"

"I don't know anything about it, Guy," PJ said, trying to avoid the subject. His stomach was growling. He looked at his noonday shadow on the ground and wondered if it was getting close to time for dinner. He had a depressing thought. Guy might not stop to eat. He wondered if he should remind him of it.

"You won't tell anybody about this will you, PJ?"

A small cloud passed between them and the sun. PJ, appreciating the momentary shade, glanced up. It made him wonder if they might get some rain. A rain would break the heat.

"Well, I'll tell you, PJ, I probably wouldn't be married to Grace right now if her momma hadn't come after me with the sheriff. She wadn't pregnant. She wadn't. She jes said she was. I think she jes wanted to git out of havin' to pick cotton and she liked that old '39 Ford coupe I had. Her whole idea of being married was driving up and down the road."

"What time is it?" Roy called. He was even further behind.

PJ turned to Stookey. "You think it's time to quit for dinner?"

21

"Time to eat," Roy shouted.

Stookey looked up at the sun and then back down at his shadow. "Naw, not yet."

"Not yet," PJ called back. Isn't that the way it goes, he thought. Here's Guy letting out a lot of stuff and there's nosy Roy back there missing every bit of it.

Guy was saying, "Grace wasn't but 15 when we first started pickin' cotton together," . . . but PJ stopped listening because it made him think about Glory Johnson, Lee Junior's younger sister, how she used to come over and pick cotton alongside and talk to him. He had liked that. He liked having somebody to work with, somebody like Glory who knew things that he didn't know anything at all about, especially about girls and women.

Roy's mentioning eating made him realize how shriveled up and empty his stomach felt. He would have to eat something soon. But Guy didn't seem to be slowing up. PJ realized he might just go on this way all day.

"I hit bottom on tiredness," Guy was saying. "Never was so worn out. Workin' all day, then comin' home and workin' all night, you know what I mean."

PJ was hoping his grandmother would look out and see them and call them in for dinner. He imagined her saying, "Guy Stookey's a good influence on those boys. Look out there. Hot as it is, they just keep on working."

Stookey shook his head. "I couldn't keep the pace she had."

This kind of talk made PJ uncomfortable. Behind them, Roy was now down on his knees. Must be sharpening the blade of his hoe, PJ thought. He felt for the metal file in his own back pocket just to check that it was still there. "Guy, my hoe's gettin' a little dull. Think we could stop and sharpen it?"

"Naw," he said, looking ahead to the end of the row. "We'll be out of here in a little bit."

Sure would like to sharpen my hoe, PJ thought. His arms ached. He wished there was some breeze.

"But I liked them ten years, PJ. I liked that woman. Sometimes I heard things. People won't tell you right out. Even if I know'd about it, I mightn't of said anything. You think that's wrong?"

22

I don't know, Guy." But PJ did know he'd like to get him a bucket of white paint and take it over to the school and paint out those things they wrote about Grace on the wall in the boys' toilet.

And the next time he heard somebody making a joke about Guy, he'd like to say to them, "Guy Stookey's a friend of mine and I'm going to tell him you said that." That ought to shut 'em up.

They got to the end of the row at the same time. PJ started to prop his hoe against the old barbed wire fence, but Guy said they couldn't quit. They couldn't leave Roy out there by himself, so they turned and started working back.

PJ's eyes quickly scanned the whole field before he saw where Roy was. He was way over by the south fence. His brother had his hoe high in the air and he was running across the cotton rows hitting at something on the ground.

"What the hell is he doing?" Guy wanted to know.

PJ didn't know for sure, but guessed Roy was over there trying to kill one of those big lizards they sometimes found out in the cotton fields. "Yeah, he's probably after one of those Gila Monsters. He's killed 'em before. That is probably what he is chasing."

PJ put his hand up to his mouth and called out loud across the field to his brother, "Roy, come back over to where you supposed to be. We're gonna help you out. Hoe fast as you can."

The two of them watched Roy stop and think for just a moment, then quickly lowered his hoe and at a fast stride headed back across the field.

"You sure you ain't heard anything, PJ?" Guy asked quietly as they hoed along Roy's row.

"About what, Guy?"

"You would tell me, wouldn't you? I know Mr. Beeman or Claire Ruth or some of them others might not tell me. But you ain't got no reason not to."

PJ said, "Honest, Guy, I don't know where she's at." But right then he made a secret vow to himself that if he could find out, he sure would tell him.

23

When they met up with Roy, the three of them picked up their hoes, put them on their shoulders and started walking in the direction of Granny Purdee's big two-story house. PJ noticed Stookey reach into his shirt pocket and pull out what was left of his biscuit. Since he just held it in his hand as he walked, PJ thought maybe Guy would have dinner with them at the big house. He hoped he would.

"Guy," Roy spoke up as he strode briskly along trying to keep up with Stookey's long steps, "I figured out what I like most about choppin' cotton."

"What's that, Roy?"

"Quittin'."

"Sounds like you, Roy."

When they walked past Pap's old tractor shed they saw Grandee standing over by the water tank underneath the windmill. She was carrying a bucket of water and had her red apron on. "I thought y'all was goin' to work right through dinner," she said.

"Them's long rows," Stookey said. "Don't like to leave a row half-done."

She told them, "Dinner's on the table."

Guy Stookey held up his biscuit. "Appreciate it, Gran, but I brought my dinner. I'll just have a little of that good water you've got, and git on back to work."

The boys ate too much. After their meal, they thanked their grandmother and went outside to sit for a while on the bare ground under the big post oak by the tractor shed. In the distance, they could see the lone figure on the far side of the cotton field, his dusty white frame nodding under the heat of the afternoon sun.

"What'd you find out?" Roy wanted to know.

"About what?"

"What was Stookey and you talking about?"

PJ looked at his brother. It came to him all of a sudden. Who was it wrote those things in the boys' toilet? Maybe it was Roy. It would have been like him to do that.

PJ got up and with his toe eased the handle of his hoe up from the ground.

"Where you goin'?" Roy wanted to know.

"I'm goin' back to work."

"We don't have to go back yet," Roy said. But PJ was already headed out toward the field with his hoe in his hand.

MAKING READY FOR THE RIVER

PJ parked Mr. Sapp's old GMC underneath the big post oak in Nettie Johnson's front yard. The truck still had the wooden side stanchions on from last winter when he and Lee Junior had been put to work cleaning up around the cotton gin, hauling off the moats and cotton burr waste that had piled up during last season.

Lee Junior Johnson was PJ's longest and best friend, and the rest of this family were like distant cousins, the kind you don't see every day but wish you did.

PJ climbed up into the back of the truck, took out the tailgate and threw down a coiled length of rope.

Lee Junior's mother Nettie was coming out the screen door of the rent house. Nettie was like a second mother to PJ, since she was the mid-wife who was there helping out on the day he was born. And, because his mother Belle was a single parent, PJ had spent almost as much time with the Johnsons as he had with his own family.

That was 14 years ago. Dr. Peyton Jackson had sent for Nettie to come help when he saw that PJ was going to have to be delivered feet first. It was a difficult birth, as almost everybody on the Prairie knew. Sometimes people still asked him about what that was like, but of course he didn't really know.

The screen door banged behind her, and Nettie quickly set down a washtub of groceries on the top step between the wisteria vine and the row of potted geraniums hanging in the drip line of the porch.

Spread out before her on the porch and further out into the yard were such items as a minnow bucket, a grubbing hoe, a foxhole shovel, a roll of rusty hog wire and bags and cardboard boxes of other things to take to the River.

The Juneteenth goat she had tied to the end post of the porch was stretching to reach the geraniums.

PJ was the one Nettie had asked to see if he could borrow Mr. Sapp's truck for the Johnson family to use to haul them and all their stuff to their annual celebration down on the Theodosa River.

At the time, PJ had wondered why they didn't just borrow his mother's car. But now that he realized how many people and how much stuff they were going to cart down to the River, he understood why they needed a truck.

"You girls don't jes stand around dere," Nettie called out to her eight-year old twin girls, Lilly and Amy. "Take dese things over to the truck and hands 'em up to Mr. PJ."

PJ never could get used to Nettie referring to him as "Mr." But he long ago had come to understand that, just to be safe, Lee Junior's mother addressed all white males that same way.

He couldn't help but remember that Lee Junior's father, the year before he was killed in a logging accident, had once called him "Master PJ." It was when PJ about 10 years old and his friend Lee Junior was 13.

The two of them were taking Junior's father something to eat where he was working in the woods with some white men. It was mid-day when they encountered Samuel Johnson sitting by himself down on the creek. Mr. Johnson was having a drink from a bottle of whiskey.

Caught by surprise, he jumped up. "You wouldn't tell on me would you Massa PJ?"

As PJ recalled, he couldn't do anything except shake his head, no.

Of course he wouldn't ever do anything like that – something that might cause Junior's father to lose his job. PJ had always been like a member of that family. This was a serious test that he passed.

After that, Sam Johnson seemed to be more at ease around him. He even joshed PJ around sometimes, being playful with him as he was with the other kids.

As for Nettie calling him "Mr. PJ," he knew there wasn't anything he could do about it. That had just become his name as far as she was concerned.

Lee Junior's sister Glory arrived from around back of the house, where she was tending a fire going under the wash pot. She gave PJ a big smile. Glory Johnson couldn't have been much over 15-years old but she carried a baby on her hip, and it was hers.

Glory was the second oldest of Nettie's five children. He didn't know her as well as he knew Lee Junior, but among Negro girls he knew Glory best. The two of them had chopped and picked cotton for PJ's grandmother and, even more often, they had picked peas and dug sweet potatoes and hauled watermelon out of the field that the Johnson family rented from their landlord, Cyrus Sapp.

Glory and he were both fast workers and, more often than not, found themselves out ahead of the rest. They each liked having the other as company. They didn't have to talk as they worked, but often did. PJ had lots of questions to ask, and he ended up telling her things he wouldn't have told anybody else. But that was before the baby.

"Would you mind holding my boy for a minute, PJ," she said, without the slightest thought that PJ might object. She just handed the baby over to him. "I got to run inside and get some trotlines and stuff from under the bed."

PJ took the baby. The child didn't have a stitch of clothing on.

Seeing what Glory had done, Nettie called across the yard, "Daughter, you should'a put a diaper on dat boy." To PJ she cautioned, "Doan let him pee on you now."

Nettie quickly turned her attention to her 8-year old twins Amy and Lilly. "You girls put down them crawdads," she scolded. "Y'all go hep Pappaw with what he doin'. He can't wrestle dat boat out from under the house all by hisself."

The twins had found the crawfish bucket. A red-striped crawfish in each hand, they were menacing each other and squawking like geese. They were using PJ like he was an object to dodge behind.

"Be careful with those things!" PJ teased the two of them. "They've got claws big enough to take a chunk out of somebody."

He liked the twins, and they liked when he came over.

Old Deef and Dumb Dunfee, as the Negro community called Nettie's grandfather, had crawled under the house with the purpose of snaking out their big flat-bottomed boat. PJ couldn't see where he was, but from the squawking and the chicken feathers flying out he guessed that the old man was in hand-to-hand combat with one of Nettie's setting hens.

"Watch them eggs," Nettie yelled through the floor of the porch. She then threw up her hands, and said to nobody: "Pappaw doan hear nothin'."

Nettie called to her six-year old son standing in the yard. "Poppy, git under dere and see dem eggs doan git broke."

Glory's baby was squirming around so much that it was hard for PJ to keep a grip on him. He saw it coming but there wasn't anything he could do about it. PJ tried to hold the naked baby out away from him, but the baby's thing was pointed right at him. The warm stream got PJ right in the chest.

"He's went and done it again," Nettie told her daughter as she came out of the house. "Mr. PJ's all wet now."

"He's a quick one," she called to PJ from the porch. There was laughter in her voice. "He'll git you ever time."

The girls were still chasing each other with the crawfish. "Hep me, PJ. Heaapp!" One twin pulled at PJ's pants, trying to hide behind him. "Doan let em git me."

PJ held onto the baby with one hand and tried to keep his pants from falling down with the other. The wetness had run down his shirt and stained the whole front of his britches.

From the porch clothesline, Glory grabbed a towel and came down into the yard to shoo her younger sisters away. "Y'all git on away. Leave PJ alone. Put them thangs back in the bucket. They all going to die."

"Here, PJ, let me takes him `fore he do somethin' else." She took the child in exchange for the towel.

Nettie called over from the porch. "We never goin' to git all dis stuff loaded up if you kids don't behave."

PJ wished Lee Junior was there now to help get the truck

loaded. He could hear Junior's old two-cylinder John Deere with the broke-over exhaust at work for a neighbor a mile away. If the Johnsons were ever going to get all these Juneteenth things hauled down to the River today, PJ realized he was going to have to take more of a role in making it happen.

The flat-bottomed wooden boat was emerging from under the house a little bit at a time. The old man was sitting on the ground pushing it with his feet.

PJ went over to help. Now that the boat was halfway out from under the house he could see that it was full of hay and covered with chicken droppings.

As it came on out into the yard, PJ reached and helped the old man get up. Together, they flipped the boat over, letting most of the nesting trash fall to the ground, before flipping it back again.

Seeing the anchor rope, PJ just picked it up and dragged the boat himself across the sandy yard to the truck. There, PJ hopped up into the back of the truck and called to one of the twins, "Lilly, would you mind handing me that rope?" He couldn't really tell if it was Lilly he was talking to, or if it was Amy. They looked just alike and he was used to using the first name that came to his mind.

With the rope, PJ was able to lift the front of the boat off the ground. Poppy came over and all three of the children helped push the boat all the way up into the truck.

He then called out to Nettie. "Now let's see if we can get that goat up here."

When Mr. Dunfee crawled out from under the house, he was a dirty mess. He and his clothes were covered with dust, hay straw and dried chicken manure. The old man stood with his hands on his hips, grinning a toothless smile as if it were the happiest day of his life.

He had on a brand-new pair of high top rubber boots. Above that, he was wearing what once must have been a pair of black dress pants, and a blue denim shirt that was open at the collar.

Around the old man's neck, half-hidden in the bushy grey-on-black hairs of his chest, was his asafetida bag on a platted string. The bag gave off a considerable odor. This, PJ knew, was the leather pouch containing what some people called devil's dung. PJ wasn't sure he knew how to spell - or even to properly pronounce – what folks in the colored community considered to be a powerful potion passed on to Mr. Dunfee by the Ancients.

The Ancients, as the local Negroes called their ancestors, first brought it to America from Africa. Asafetida was supposed to ward off diseases and evil spirits. PJ had even heard of white folks asking the old man to prepare this remedy for them, but PJ didn't personally know anybody, black or white, other than Mr. Dunfee, who wore one of these smelly bags.

When PJ had gone to their landlord's house on a Sunday to see about using the truck, Cyrus Sapp invited him to come up onto the porch. "Son, come on in and rest a minute," he said, pointing to a chair. "I'll get you a glass of ice water."

"No sir, that's all right. I'm not thirsty," he said, even though he was. He had just run a mile and a half in the midday sun, and sweat was beginning to show through his khaki shirt and pants. "I won't take but a minute." He remained standing on the top two steps shaded by the overhang of the porch. The coolness felt good on his bare feet.

Mr. Sapp went inside and returned with a glass of water anyway, and he stood there just inside the porch while the boy drank it from the steps.

Mr. Sapp was wearing a freshly starched shirt even though he wasn't wearing shoes. The thing about Mr. Sapp was that he was always clean. PJ could see now that even when he was at home relaxing, his pants were neatly pressed with a front crease that went all the way up to his belt.

PJ's brother Roy had bet him that they wouldn't ever catch Mr. Sapp without a pencil in his front shirt pocket. Sure enough, even though it was a Sunday, PJ saw that his landlord had two pencils stuck into his plastic shirt protector.

"He sleeps with those pencils," Roy had said. "You can bet on that."

31

The outside appearance of the Sapp home was as neat as Mr. Sapp himself. The residence was made almost entirely of red brick, with only the windowsills and the trim painted white. PJ was sure that this was the only brick house on Sandy Prairie.

Mr. Sapp watered his yard to make the grass grow. PJ didn't know of anybody else who planted grass, or even wanted grass to grow in their yard. Weeds, wiregrass, and cockleburs were all that would survive the hot, dry summers out in the fields and pastures. But in his yard Mr. Sapp planted, fertilized and watered San Augustine grass that was thick as a doormat and green all year long.

The brick home with its green yard and painted white fence stood out to passersby like something you would see in a magazine.

At the road entrance, Mr. Sapp had installed an iron cattle guard, a wide span of evenly-spaced rails that he could drive over but no cow would want to cross for fear of getting a foot caught.

That made good sense to PJ. Mr. Sapp doesn't have to take the time to get out to open a yard gate, and then close it again after he passes through it.

Nearly everybody's cows get out sooner or later, and get chased up and down the road by people like him. With all that green grass, without the cattle guard, some of them were bound to end up in Mr. Sapp's yard. PJ didn't really know Mrs. Sapp, but he was sure she would not appreciate those big juicy cow biscuits fertilizing her flower beds.

PJ had never actually been inside the house. He had heard that Mrs. Sapp had furnished it with a modern-type furniture, the kind that people on the Prairie would have been uncomfortable sitting on. But then, he had never heard of Mrs. Sapp inviting people over.

Cyrus Sapp owned quite a bit of property. In addition to the house Belle, PJ and Roy lived in, he also owned the Crossroads store, which was painted white, and the cotton gin and seed house, which were covered with unpainted tin.

Mr. Sapp had also bought several farms and two large sections of former longleaf pine cutover between the Theodosa

River bottom and the flat upland that nearly everybody referred to as the Sandy Prairie.

The land and house that Nettie Johnson and her family lived in also belonged to Mr. Sapp. Lee Junior and his family would normally have worked their place on the halves, which in most cases meant that they would split their crops with their landlord at the end of the year.

While it was common practice for tenant farmer families to run up a bill for the provisions they bought at the store during spring and summer, and divide proceeds from crops raised at the end of the season, the Johnson family no longer did that.

The Nettie Johnson arrangement was somewhat different. Now that her son Lee Junior was old enough to manage a truck crop operation, the family was mostly growing vegetables, plus cantaloupes and watermelons, and some flowers and plants and selling them in town at the farmers' market. And they made special deliveries directly to stores.

Unlike cotton and peanuts, the growing season for collard greens and turnips, vine crops such as purple hull peas and melons, and root crops like Irish potatoes and sweet potatoes those food items were available from early spring to late fall. With cash to pay, the Johnson family rarely needed to run up a bill at the Crossroads store.

PJ often dropped by to give the Johnson family a hand, for which they nearly always sent him home with some eggs, a mess of greens, several ears of sweet corn or a watermelon. Sometimes he bought with his own money their fresh-shelled peas and delivered them to families around the Prairie, especially to the elderly and the shut-in people.

Sometimes those folks paid him more than the peas were worth, and sometimes he wouldn't take any money at all.

Although Lee Junior was 17 years old, and they were three years apart in age, it didn't seem to matter. They appreciated one another almost as if they were brothers, which in a sense they were since their mother Nettie Johnson was there to bring them into the world.

As Lee Junior was now the sole working male of the Johnson household, and a successful truck farmer who owned his own tractor, and could hire people to transport his marketable goods to town, nearly everyone–including Mr. Sapp–treated him as if he were a grown man.

After Lee Junior's father had been killed in a logging accident, Mr. Sapp took a helpful interest in the future of the Johnson family. One important thing that PJ learned that their landlord did was to order seed and fertilizer for Lee Junior through the store, and to personally loan him the farm equipment he needed to get started growing food crops.

On the occasion of the colored folks' Juneteenth celebration, PJ never thought for one minute that Mr. Sapp would mind if he came to his house asking to borrow the bobtail truck. He and Junior both had done work for him using that truck on multiple occasions.

"Where are they going to have it?" Mr. Sapp wanted to know.

"On the River. They always like to go down there."

"They've got a goat?"

"Mr. Dunfee's been feeding one out on the bottle."

"A little one, is it?"

"It's not too big but I don't really think its a young one."

Mr. Sapp smiled and said, "Trying to tender him up, I guess." With his gold-rimmed glasses in his pointing hand, he motioned toward the machine shop at the cotton gin. "You may find you'll have to charge up the battery on that old truck before it'll start. You know where the charger is kept."

"Nettie says to tell you they sure appreciate this."

"I know that."

PJ was already down the steps and headed for the cattle guard when Mr. Sapp called out to him, "PJ, be sure you've got enough gas. Fill the truck up there at the shop."

"Yes Sir, I know where it's at."

"And PJ," Mr. Sapp called, "pick out a couple of cases of soft drinks at the store. Tell Bee to put them on my bill."

"Yes Sir, I'll do that."

PJ turned again to go, but Mr. Sapp had something else to tell him. "Wish Nettie and her family a happy June Nineteenth for me, will you?"

His landlord had come all the way out into the yard. In one of his hands, he was holding the glasses he was polishing. In the other, he held a clean white handkerchief. Out in the sun without his narrow brim fedora hat, Cyrus Sapp looked smaller and pale.

Walking backwards out into the road, PJ called back, "I'll see if Nettie can't save you some." PJ understood that returning with some of that good barbecue would please Mr. Sapp a lot.

Back at Nettie's place, little Poppy had climbed up onto the back of the truck. "Is you goin' to stay all night, PJ?"

With help from the old grandfather, PJ managed to wrestle the goat up into the back of the gin shop truck. He and Poppy then practically had to drag the struggling goat up to the front of the truck bed, where they tied him down so he wouldn't be able to jump out. "I aim to do that, Poppy."

"Den I's goin' to too." He called to Nettie. "I's goin' to stay all night, Momma."

"All right. But you got to go git your pallet."

The twin girls started to climb up into the back of the truck to join their little brother, but Nettie called them down. "Tomorrow is when the women folk go," Nettie said. "Just the mens is going down to the River this evening. That's the old way."

Poppy asked PJ, "Do they haves to kill the goat?"

PJ didn't say anything.

Poppy was emphatic. "I doan wants them to kill no goat." His sister Glory was on the ground handing up the paddles to the boat. "It wouldn't be Juneteenth," she said, "if there wasn't no goat."

Poppy asked, "Is you going to eat some of him, PJ?"

"I expect so."

The old man was waving his hand at the sun. Nettie called out to PJ, "Pappaw wants to git over there to the River and put the fire on. Poppy, you help out now."

PJ was hoping Lee Junior would show up before they left, but it looked like he wasn't going to.

The girls brought over the mens' bedding, the big skillet, the can of lard, the bait bucket and some fishing line off the porch and handed them up into the truck.

The old man had disappeared to around the back of the house and came out dragging several sheets of rusty tin roofing and some chicken wire. PJ helped him pick up and shove these into the back of the truck.

"Look-a-here," Poppy exclaimed from the back of the truck. "Where'd all these soda waters come from, PJ?"

"Soda waters?" The twins jumped off the porch and ran around the side of the truck. "Is they for us?"

"Yes, they are," PJ spoke up. "Mr. Sapp sent them as a present for your holiday celebration."

"Can we has one now?"

"They are all hot right now," PJ said. "They'll be better when they're cold."

"Them's for the 'teenth," Nettie scolded.

"Don't worry," PJ reassured them. "They'll be there when you come tomorrow."

CATFISHING ON THE RIVER

June 19th wasn't officially a holiday. PJ and everybody else knew that it wasn't, but it was celebrated as a day off by whites as well as colored.

PJ had heard white folks reasoning that since black folks wouldn't work on June 19, they might as well take that day off too, and then nobody would have any basis for complaining about working on the 4th of July.

The 4th of July is an official holiday, but nobody in the farming community will take off because it comes at a time when everybody needs to be working their crops from sunup to sundown.

On the 19th of June, work to be done or not, nobody argues: it is a day of rest and relaxation. And that is exactly what most people did on Juneteenth.

For his black brother Lee Junior, June 19 was a big day in more ways than one. It was his birthday. Some in the Negro community held the view that Lee Junior's being born on Proclamation Day was a sign: he was going to be a leader among his people.

Lee Junior didn't admit to that. But PJ thought, as a lot of people did, if there ever was a Negro who would amount to something, Lee Junior certainly would.

"Is that everything?" PJ asked, as he hopped down to the ground from the bed of Mr. Sapp's truck.

"The rest you kin git later," Nettie spoke from the yard. "Y'all go ahead on afore it gits dark."

Poppy came up behind PJ as he was fastening the tailgate.

"Where you goin' to sleep?" he asked somewhat timidly.

"Maybe I won't sleep. Maybe I'll just stay up all night, Poppy."

"Den maybe I won't sleep neither. . . But ifs you do sleep, could I sleep wid you?"

"You sure could."

"Boy," he sighed.

PJ climbed up into the driver's seat, and pulled Poppy up after him. The boy settled into the middle between PJ and the grandfather. The old man had already closed the door on his side and was sitting forward in the seat looking straight on. The way he was staring, it was if the River was just ahead and he wanted to be the first one to see it.

Without thinking, PJ asked the old man, "Have we got everything?"

Mr. Dunfee had never heard a word in his life, but people talked to him just like he could hear. And somehow there was the basis of communication. In this case, with his left hand he made several short motions for PJ to start the truck and git going, right now. He did this without taking his eyes off the destination he had in his head.

PJ leaned out the window. "Nettie, tell Junior I'll be back to get him a little after dark."

He wasn't really surprised that his friend didn't come in from the field a little early, but considering it was the eve of Juneteenth, he had hoped he might.

PJ had to press hard to get the clutch all the way to the floor. He turned on the key. When he stomped down on the starter with the other foot, the truck started right up. In low gear, he made a wide slow turn across a half-dozen rows of purple hull peas before he got the old GMC straightened up and headed out toward the road.

He could have backed up and not run down some of Nettie's cash crop, but with no side mirrors he couldn't see that well behind and didn't want to take the chance that he would run over somebody.

The truck headed south on the main road. PJ sat up on the edge of his seat to get a good view of where he was going, pressing his elbow outward in the window to make himself look taller than he was.

When he drove past the school grounds and turned off the road at the store, he was looking every minute out of the corner of his eyes to see if there was anybody there noticing.

He waved at Joey Lou Truehaw, who came past pulling a side–delivery rake, and he thought maybe Itchy Gates, who was out back of her house hanging up clothes with her mother, might have seen him going by, but he wasn't sure.

PJ felt the satisfaction of knowing that Mr. Sapp had confidence in him. That made jobs such as this one all the more important for him to do well.

It took them a little more than an hour to get down to the River going the back way. Poppy kept urging him to speed up. "Faster, PJ. Faster. Make de wind blow." But he drove in a slower gear the greater part of the way because he wanted to be really careful.

The old logging road was mostly just one lane. He was afraid he might meet a car or truck coming the other way. A road grader had been through since the last rain, but the sand seemed deep and worrisome. He tried to keep the front wheels of the GMC straddling the center of the road.

The Cutover on either side was grown up in a tall mass of vegetation so thick that you had to imagine, or work your way in there to see for yourself, where the great stumps were.

To PJ, the stumps were the proof that an ancient forest once thrived in this place. A longleaf pine tree stump will not rot. If someone wanted to see just how old the trees were before the big mills from the north came and took the native pines away, all they needed to do was to climb up and count the growth rings on some of these big tree stumps.

When the road forked, PJ paused the truck. He knew they were inside lumber company property and he thought they had been traveling on Old Dirty Creek Road, but now he wasn't sure.

The grandfather made a gesture toward the right, so they went in that direction. But a wire cross-fence soon blocked their further passage.

Mr. Dunfee clearly did not like the idea of the fence being there. He looked to the left and right and turned around in his seat to look behind. His eyes were squinting like he was trying to remember. He shook his head. With no teeth, his chin stuck out so far it almost touched his nose. He turned to PJ and made a series of sharp forward gestures as if PJ should drive right through the fence.

"You think we're allowed to go this way?" PJ asked him. Mr. Dunfee waved for him to turn around, which PJ managed to do with some difficulty, because of the deep sand.

They crept along looking for what might be another way in. This time, they found a wire gap that opened to a recently used logging road with a lane heading southwest. Mr. Dunfee seemed to think it was the way to go.

PJ asked Poppy, "You want to try opening that gate for us?" The old man got out with him, and together they took the wire barrier down and pulled it back out of the way. PJ drove the truck through.

"Y'all wants it closed?" Poppy asked.

"We better close it," PJ called back. The old man and the boy refastened the wire, climbed back in, and they started out again.

The logging road took them through a grove of hardwood trees. Driving in the woods made it seem late in the day even though, by the sun, it must have been no later than three or four o'clock. The branches of the old water oaks scraped at the sides of the truck, which made Poppy scream with pretended fear.

His excitement reminded PJ of the way the twins and Poppy screamed when he went with the Johnson family to the County Fair and they all rode the Ferris wheel. It looked dangerous but it really wasn't.

PJ knew they must be getting close to the River when the old man sat erect in his seat, peering forward. His mouth was open; his eyes were intensely black. When they pulled to a stop at a place that looked like an old campsite, Mr. Dunfee patted the dash of the truck with his hand in appreciation, as if it was the nape of an old mule that had safely brought them home.

Once they were at the River, after PJ helped unload the truck and wrestle the goat over to where they tied him up to a tree, PJ felt like an outsider. The message he got from the old man's behavior was that this white boy was no longer needed, and now that he had got them to the River, he was just in the way. That was the sum of it.

Mr. Dunfee rejected any further offers to assist, and shooed him away as if he were no more than a chicken. The old man was clearly in charge, and this was his event.

The grandfather got down on his knees and, by himself, dug a hole in the sandy ground with a grubbing hoe. He then positioned the old sheets of tin roofing around the sides of this hole and laid a metal frame over it.

He sent Poppy out to gather dry wood, so PJ went with him, helping him find an old oak that was dead and losing its limbs. But just as soon as they had brought up several arm loads of smaller kindling, Mr. Dunfee dismissed PJ from the area and split most of the bigger pieces himself.

With not much help from Poppy, and no help from PJ, the grandfather killed the goat and strung him upside down on a low branch of a hickory tree where he gutted it. For over an hour, the old man and young Poppy sat on the bank of the River with their feet in the water, cleaning a tub of goat entrails

Old Deaf and Dumb Dunfee wasn't supposed to be able to hear or speak, but there sure was an awful lot of jabbering going on, and it wasn't coming just from Poppy. The words were not anything PJ could make out, but to him it sounded like two people talking, and some of it was like chanting.

PJ was feeling useless. He wondered whether Lee Junior would tell him what this whole Juneteenth-at-the-River was about without his having to ask.

To pass the time, he climbed up on top of the truck cab where it was a little cooler and the gnats and mosquitoes were not as thick. From his backpack, he got out a pencil and some paper with which he made notes that would help him remember what they did today. And he made some quick pencil drawings in his notebooks.

Bored with that, PJ picked up Poppy's homemade nigger shooter and walked off down to a little slough that ran into the River. His idea was to plunk log turtles resting in the quiet water. It was something to do until it was time for him to drive the truck back up to the Prairie to get Lee Junior.

He was down there for a while, but he was getting hungry

from the first smell of cooking meat. He kept looking back up toward the fire, thinking somebody might call to him. And sure enough they did.

The old goat master walked out away from the fire and signaled him over. Pointing to his forefinger, which he crooked in the shape of a fishhook, he waved PJ toward the River.

With no more instruction than that, PJ understood that the old black man was ready to set out fishing lines in the River. Whether or not PJ would be asked to go out with him on the River in his boat was not clear.

From the truck, PJ went and gathered up the bait bucket and the white cotton trotlines that had the fish hooks attached and everything else that seemed to have to do with night fishing. He followed the grandfather and grandson Poppy down to the thin sandbar that gave easy entrance to the River. That was where the three of them had anchored the old flat bottom boat upon their arrival in the late afternoon, leaving two paddles in the boat.

The first thing the old man did when they got down to the water's edge was to hand PJ something wrapped in a piece of newspaper. PJ immediately knew what it was, and took it as a kind of peace offering.

"Thank you, Sir," and quickly tucked the package into his backpack, knowing now was not the time to try Mr. Dunfee's barbecue.

The grizzled grandfather waded out into the water right up to his knees, with water pouring in over his high-top rubber boots. He stretched to settle the coal oil lantern into the bottom of the boat. Holding the craft steady, he motioned for PJ to get in first up front, and for Poppy to climb into the middle. Then, Mr. Dunfee practically fell over into the whole back section.

With his paddle, the grandfather pushed them off. It took a few minutes of floating around in a circle and getting crosswise to the current before PJ caught on to the old man's way of making the boat go where he wanted it to. PJ had never done this before.

Mr. Dunfee, sitting in the back, gently tapped his paddle on the side he wanted PJ to pull on. With the old man paddling on one side, and PJ on the other, they managed to get the boat moving smoothly forward, with no talking at all.

They were heading up-river and the current was against them. PJ thought how much easier two strong paddlers working in tandem made the job, when one was pulling on the left and the other was simultaneously pulling on the right.

From this act of cooperative effort, he learned how easy it was to row a boat upstream, and learning something new always made PJ feel good.

It took them about an hour to set the trotlines. PJ had heard about fishing for catfish using trotlines, but this was the first time he saw how it worked. Each line consisted of a strong cotton cord about ten yards long with a dozen or so shorter cords coming off each line, spaced about a yard apart. Each had a large fishhook attached to the end.

Mr. Dunfee headed their boat in the direction of an old live oak that had fallen into the River, and PJ tied the first line to a dead branch of the tree. Then, after paddling about 10 yards further upstream, they connected the other end of the cord to an overhanging limb of another tree leaning out over the water.

Further up River they set three more trotlines, taking care to select the quieter places along the River's edge where the fish would come up to feed.

Since PJ was up front in the boat, he was the one to attach the main line to a sturdy snag or limb, while the old man kept the boat steady against the current. As they moved forward, little Poppy helped his grandfather bait each of the hooks with grub worms, crawfish and cut up pieces of yellow perch.

Each set they dropped into the water behind them. They marked the location of each line with a strip of cloth torn from an old bed sheet so they would be able find each trotline later when they came back to see if they had caught anything.

The moon had not yet come out and it was near dark when they got back to the camp. Without speaking, they tied the boat up to a well-anchored huckleberry bush at the sandbar. Mr. Dunfee hurried back to check on his barbecue and PJ and Poppy got in the truck and headed for the Prairie.

Lee Junior was waiting for them when PJ and Poppy pulled

into the yard in Mr. Sapp's truck. The girls had lots of questions as they helped the boys load up the remaining provisions that would be needed at the celebration tomorrow.

The three males - Junior, Poppy and PJ - left immediately knowing that the old grandfather was down at the River alone.

"Well, Poppy, how is it on the River?" Lee Junior asked of his little brother, once they were in the truck and going. Poppy was sitting between Junior's long legs in the front seat of the truck.

PJ was again the driver, but this time it was night. The stars were out, but not giving off much light. He couldn't see any farther ahead than the truck lights bouncing on the sandy lane. Lee Junior's arm was out the window. The vent was wide open so he could catch the night breeze. The lights of the dash gave a green cast to the black faces. Poppy thought before he answered. "I doan likes it."

"Was you afred?"

"I wadn't afred," Poppy insisted. "I jes doan likes it."

Lee asked, "Did you watch how Papaw killed that goat?"

"With just his hands, that's how he killed it," Poppy seemed distressed about that.

PJ turned to Lee Jr., wanting to enter the conversation. Because he was curious, he asked, "Smothered it? Is that the way he does it?"

"What'd it look like to you?"

"I couldn't really tell. I stayed over by the truck. I could see your Papaw was bent over, like he was looking the goat in the eye, and that goat was a lot more cooperative than I would have expected. I saw it getting shaky in the knees. Then, I saw it just fell over."

"What surprised me was that your Pap sat down on top of him and put his hands up around its nose. When he got up, that goat never moved again. I assumed it was dead, and it really was."

"He didn't let you help any, did he?" Lee Junior asked the question as if he already knew the answer.

"I offered to," PJ told him. "But your Papaw was real agitated about anything like that. He waved me away, all the way, away from there," PJ used his right hand to demonstrate. "I was standing off to the side pretty near the whole time. . . . Now Poppy here, he figured in it."

"Yes, dat's de old way," Lee Junior said.

"It is?"

"It has to be a male. Ye see, by tradition, de mens is the onliest ones who can prepare the goat," he said.

PJ turned and looked at Lee Junior, who was looking right at him with a big grin on his face. "I guess he couldn't tell I wasn't a girl, is that it?"

Junior kidded him back. "I guess you just wasn't lucky enough to be born black."

At the edge of the small clearing along the River bank, PJ stopped the truck but left the headlights on. Mr. Dunfee came out into the light. The old man's skin was ink black and glistening wet with sweat. PJ could see that his clothes were soaking wet as well. The grandfather was waving his arms for the boys to turn the headlights off, so PJ did. The only light out there then came from the roaring fire the old man had going down by the River.

PJ could see that some of the goat meat, now almost the color of charcoal, was spread out on the hog wire frame he had assembled over a second pit he had dug nearby.

The grandfather was carrying coals from the fire and shoveling them down into the pit. The drippings from the meat and from the sauce popped and sizzled, filling the cavity of the River and the woods beyond with a heavy sweet smoke.

Once Lee Junior was there, the old goat master seemed to relax. PJ thought to himself that Mr. Dunfee ought to teach Junior how to do all this. He really was too old to be trying to do this all by himself.

When he was ready to run the lines in the River, the grandfather motioned to them. PJ could tell that Junior was excited to be going out in the boat.

Junior confided to PJ, "You know, I been doing this nearly every year since I was Poppy's age. For me, running the trotlines at night is one of the best parts."

As they walked over, Junior was grinning as he looked at

PJ, and shook his finger at him. "Now, if you haven't gone and messed this all up, I bet this time we'll catch us a big mess of catfish."

PJ knew Junior was joshing him, and had an inclination to say something back, but stopped himself. What he was thinking of saying was something like "all the white perch in the River that we might catch are going to be scared off by your black face," but he didn't because this was not the right time or place.

The flat-bottom boat was where they had left it, tied up in a thick mass of lily pads in a shallow slough off the main channel. PJ was once more directed to sit up-front and Lee Junior sat in the middle. Poppy was settled into the bottom of the boat between his brother's legs. The old man took his place in the back and pushed off.

This time, PJ felt a lot more confident about what he was supposed to be doing. He got satisfaction from the fact that he could now pull his paddle in perfect sync with the oarsman at the rear, without looking back and without a single word being exchanged between them.

The moon was coming out and the light was good enough for PJ to see the cypress knees sticking up through the mud. To him, they always looked like little monks at prayer.

They paddled out to where the slow current of the river caught them, and momentarily shoved them back. They had to work to make their way upstream.

The heat of the day was gone. A breeze came gently down the River, stroking the cypress branches along the banks and turning slowly the shiny sides of the dogwood leaves in the moonlight. The gust of wind momentarily held them and their boat, pushing them back, before it whispered past.

The River was full of noisy quiet. There were no trucks to be heard on the road, no silage cutters or hay balers or cotton gins roaring in the night, no one singing or calling out. But it was noisy, unbelievably noisy, just the same.

The sounds they made, the paddles pulling in the water, khaki sleeves brushing against wood, their very breathing echoing in the River channel, was nothing compared to the din around them.

Ancient bullfrogs with labored voices grouched and groaned and complained for as far as the River was long. Tree frogs, green peepers and katydids, millions and millions of them, spared no effort to outdo each other.

Mosquitoes like tiny chain saws came out of black space to light on their ears. Far in the woods a panther screamed. Bullgators bellowed in sloughs where man may never have been. Night birds he didn't know the name of made lonesome pleas. PJ thought how silly it was that people would go on about how quiet it was down on the River.

Without speaking, PJ pointed toward the fallen tree. Now that the moon was coming out, they could see more clearly the white marker and the cotton cord set earlier. The four short lines were now all within sight.

This time, PJ had a clearer idea of what he was expected to do to fish for channel cat. Just beyond the tree snag, he grasped the fishing line and lifted it a little at a time. By pulling on it, he was able to draw the boat forward. He thought he felt something more than the resistance of the line. But he wasn't sure.

"I think we got one," PJ whispered. He didn't know why he whispered; it just seemed like he should.

"What is it, PJ?" Poppy was leaning forward trying to get a look.

"We'll see," he whispered back. There was nothing, not even any bait left on the first two hooks, but after that, there was definitely something. "Yeah, we got him," PJ said a little louder now.

The dripping line passed over the boat as he pulled it along. "Hold on a minute," Lee Junior said. "Let me bait these here hooks while we at it." He hooked two crawfish through the tails. They dangled and silently thrashed as the boat moved on and the bait submerged with the line.

"Pass 'em back. I'll take 'em off," Lee Junior said softly.

PJ was startled and jumped when he saw it. "It's not no fish," he said, falling easily into the colored way of speaking. At first, he thought it was a snake because it had a head like a snake, but then he saw it wasn't. "It's a turtle," he said.

With some effort, PJ held the line up so that the turtle was all the way out of the water. Its neck stretched half again as his body was long. Its flippers were going up and down like it was swimming in the air. Poppy shrunk away in fear.

"Hit's a soft-shell," Lee Junior said. "That's a good 'un."

When the turtle on the line came past Poppy, the boy was frightened. "Lets him go," he cried as he moved out of the way toward the front of the boat.

"Set down, Poppy," Lee Junior told him with a firm voice. "You goin' to fall out."

"Doan puts him in here," Poppy pleaded.

"Hit's all right," Lee Junior said. "Gimmy that toesack."

PJ threw him the burlap bag from under his seat. Lee Junior held up the line so the turtle was hanging over the boat. He slipped the open bag underneath. With his free hand, he got out his pocketknife and cut the hook from the line. The turtle fell into the bag, the hook still in its mouth.

"You keeps him back there," Poppy insisted.

Lee Junior reassured him. "I got him right here with me," he said with a smile.

"Tie somethin' 'round that sack," Poppy told him. "I doan wants him crawlin' out and comin' over here."

"Momma will sure be happy to see this one," Lee Junior said.

From the other three lines they got four channel cat, one of them weighing at least four pounds, and a large white perch.

They let the current slowly take them on the way back. The heat was being sucked out of the River, and a light mist rode with them on the water.

PJ rolled down his sleeves and hugged his arms to his body as the cooler air settled around them.

A water snake, its head held higher than a moccasin's, swam toward them, then turned and swam the other way.

Bats darted and dipped into the quiet surface of the River, breaking the reflection of the Milky Way above. Poppy fell asleep in the bottom of the boat, the minnow bucket between his legs, his head resting against PJ's back.

They ran the lines for the last time just about daybreak and removed the fishing line, rolling each set into a ball for easy transport back to the Johnson's family home, where it would be stored until the next big trip down to the Theodosa River, when they would celebrate "Juneteenth" in another year.

CELEBRATING JUNETEENTH

On the morning of June 19, 1950, two cars and a pickup load of black folks made their way through the longleaf pine Cutover of Theodosa County and joined the Johnson men down at the River. Their mission was to celebrate their most important holiday.

Some of these people PJ did not know. One of the cars was long and black and shiny, like a hearse. The people that got out were dressed in their best go-to-meeting clothes.

PJ recognized and spoke to Mr. Tom and Miss Mary. Mr. Tom had brought cotton in a wagon pulled by two mules to the gin last season, so PJ knew who he was, and he had sometimes seen Miss Mary walking between the store and the Arlyn Jones place, where they were share croppers.

PJ met for the first time Petite Fontonot, the legendary liar and storyteller, whom he had so often heard talked about. And, of course, Nettie and the girls came with the others. They came bearing fishing poles and folding chairs and dishpans full of food, smiling a lot, taking pleasure in each other, hugging and holding hands, giggling among themselves.

They all paraded by the barbecue pit and paid their respects to Mr. Dunfee. They made a big to-do about how they could "smell that goat a'cooking a mile away," and how fitting a tribute it was to have a roast on Juneteenth prepared by the "goat master" who had received his knowledge from the Ancients.

And the kids were saying, "When we goin' to eat?" And the parents were saying, as if they were repeating something they had heard a long time ago and needed to remind them of, "Chile, it be done when the sun's high in the sky. Not before."

Mr. Dunfee, lit up like all his lost children had come home, whet his butcher knife on a rock and sliced off a little taste for everybody, children and all.

"Mmmmm. Tender," they said.

"Taste that sauce," they said.

"Mr. Dunfee, this is sho' 'nuff the best you ever done."

PJ sat to the side and watched. Glory Johnson noticed him and came over with her baby on her arm.

"You didn't bring a fishin' pole?" she asked him.

"I'm not much of a fisherman," he told her.

"I'm not neither," she said smiling, as if it didn't surprise her they had that in common.

The baby reached out like he wanted PJ to take him. "PJ don't want to have nothin' to do with you," she said, putting the baby on her hip.

"This is your big day, I guess," he said.

"I guess so. . ." She studied him for a moment. "You looks like you needs some sleep."

"I'm all right."

"Ye ought to go lay down over there in the truck and get some sleep."

"I might in a little bit."

Glory looked around like she was trying to think of something. "Last year when we come down here there was lots of mayhaws."

"I haven't seen any."

"We could go look for some?"

PJ thought for a minute. "Naw, I guess not."

"We could go down to the sandbar. Maybe we could dig some mussels."

"I'll just stay around here," he said.

"It's not any good you standin' over here by yourself," she told him. "Come on, I'll get you to meet some of these people."

They walked along the River's edge and watched the pole fishermen get settled into serious talking and relaxing. Teet Fontonot had a cane pole you could put together in sections to make it as long as you wanted. He was as black as the marbles in a set of Chinese checkers and wore white painters' overalls with no shirt, a wide-brimmed felt hat with an eagle feather in it, and a pair of lace-up army boots.

Teet was telling some story about the time he was chief accountant of the Royal Bank of Paris. Glory and PJ stopped for a while and listened. Nobody believed that Teet had done the things he said he had, but they just let him go on.

That bothered PJ. It didn't seem right that people should sit and listen to one untruth after another. But they did. And they seemed to enjoy it.

PJ wondered if he himself would now go home and tell people how he met Teet Fontonot, the famous liar, and pass on all the outlandish things he had heard Teet say. He didn't think he would. But he did notice, for his own satisfaction, that there really were two gold stars in Teet's front teeth, just like people said.

They found Mr. Tom and Lee Junior sharing the same piece of shade. Mr. Tom, whom PJ had never ever heard say anything more than "Yas Suh" and "No Suh," was, with considerable enthusiasm, telling Lee Junior about his experience logging with oxen. Neither one of them was paying the least attention to their fishing.

"Dem old bulls must've weighed sixteen eighteen hundred pounds," Mr. Tom was saying. "Not necessary to put a line on any of 'em. Lots a'power, they had. Now, a bogged-down truck, thems hard to get loose once ye let 'em get offin all that muck of the River bottom. Jes take two three yoke of them ox, that'll get 'er out. Theys stronger than a big bulldozer, yes they is. Now, I muled all my life. When that mule bogs up to he belly, he just up and quits right there. Them bull teams don't do that. They pulls on through, you see."

Mr. Tom couldn't have weighed more than a hundred and twenty pounds himself. PJ found it hard to imagine a man as light and soft-mannered as Mr. Tom ever being able to handle any animal that weighed nearly a ton.

"He done took yo bobber and gone, Junior," Glory pointed out to her brother. "You best pull 'em out 'fore he done swallow your hook."

"Well look at that," Junior said turning back around. "'Scuse me a minute, Mr. Tom. Looks like somethin's threatnin' my worm."

Mr. Tom didn't let up talking. He just switched his attention to PJ and to Glory, who looked interested and were still listening. "I was with them fellers pulled all that cypress out of this here River bottom after the big cyclone come through here. You too young to 'member dat. But it was a mess all up and down this

River. Trees layin' over every which way." Mr. Tom interlocked his fingers to show how the trees were all jumbled up.

"Hot," he said. "It was the hottest I ever seed it in these woods. When the bulls come unhitched, they heads right for the slough. They needs to cool off, you see. I goes over and waits a little bit. Then I shows my whip and they come on right up out of there, like they was kittens."

PJ stayed to listen not just because it was something he wanted to know about, which it was, but because Mr. Tom seemed to need to tell to tell his story to somebody who might believe it.

Lee Junior pulled his line out of the water and held up a small brown catfish for Mr. Tom to see. "You think he's too little to keep?"

Mr. Tom didn't answer. The vision of the big bulls of his past life seemed to float in front of him.

"Scuse me, Mr. Tom. I think I'll go look for a stringer." Lee Junior patted him on the shoulder. "We'll talk some more later."

Miss Mary was the one who was supposed to be the talker. Maybe Mr. Tom didn't get much of a chance at home. Or maybe, just being here on the River set him off. Maybe he just needed somebody, somebody like Lee Junior, Glory or himself who would listen.

PJ observed that just because a person is quiet doesn't mean that they don't know anything. There may be something valuable that person can teach you.

Lee Junior walked over with PJ and Glory and the baby to where the man who came in the big car sat spraddled out on a plaid wool blanket. Junior introduced him as the Revered Lovsey Light. Mr. Light seemed especially fond of Lee Junior and reached out and held his hand and looked him over a long time.

Reverend Light carried a close resemblance to a goggle-eyed perch. His eyes bulged out so that it made you want to take your finger and see if you could push them back in.

The Reverend Light owned his own funeral home in Shreveport. He gave PJ one of his cards. It had a picture of Jesus holding up a lamp.

The Reverend passed around a jar of chocolate drops and invited them to all sit down. "Takes two," he insisted when PJ took only one, but did not sit.

The Reverend's shoes were off, and his blue suit coat was folded neatly beside a coffee can of grub worms. PJ kept looking at the man's feet. They were about five inches across at the toes. His new-looking dress shoes were long and narrow, maybe a size triple-A. The shoes couldn't have been more than an inch wide at the very tip. It made no sense to PJ how that man's feet could fit in those shoes.

"PJ, I would be pleased if you would sit aside me here," the pastor said, patting the blanket spread on the ground around him. "Lee Junior's mother has done told me about you. And she asked that I give you my blessing."

PJ was surprised by what the man said. He didn't know exactly what a blessing might involve and he did not sit down.

"Miss Nettie, she done explained to me about how you come into this world. And now that I has met you, I feel at ease telling you somethin' that no one else is goin' to tell you.

A blessing is a small thing I do, but I now know that this is a very important moment. What I will say to you now you will remember for all the days of your life."

Being respectful, PJ knelt slowly down in front of the Reverend. What he was feeling was a different kind of emotion, a sudden flood of curiosity coming from his head and real fear coming from his belly.

Still on the blanket, the Pastor rose to his knees and gave full attention to PJ. He took both of PJ's hands in his own. "Son, this blessin' I give has to do with who you are and who you will grow up to be. It is somethin' that you already knows, but perhaps you do not yet fully understand, 'cause you are still young."

PJ could do nothing but nod his head in quiet and reverent assent, for the current flowing between this preacher and himself was like electricity.

"If'n you had'a been born in Africa to the black race, PJ, your name would be Mussunda." He explained, "In Kimbundu language, Mussunda is the name given to the boy who is born feet first."

He spoke gently and sincerely. "I understand that it is your nature to have a kind heart, and that you are restless in your search for knowledge. I would say to you and this is my blessing, young Mussunda: if you let your heart be your guide and let your feet take you, few will ever be able to keep up with you."

From behind him, he heard the voice of his friend Lee junior say, "Amen to that, Reverend."

As quickly, the spell was broken. He heard the large man on the blanket say out loud for everyone to hear, but still speaking to him: "PJ, this here's a very important day. Do you know that?"

"Yes sir, I know it."

"What you know 'bout this here day?"

"It's Emancipation Proclamation Day, to celebrate the freeing of the African slaves."

"It sho' 'is. And what else?"

"It's Lee Junior's birthday."

"Dat's right. And what else?"

He couldn't think of anything else. Was it the reunion of black folks he was thinking of?

"Well, I is goin' to take the liberty to speak on it now in your presence. It's somethin' that relates to my own family. Lee Junior, he don't know about it neither, 'cause the onliest ones knows 'bout it is Misses Light and me and an old man who don't talk." He nodded his head and moved his hand in gentle acknowledgment in the direction of Mr. Dunfee.

Glory's baby was caressing his mother's bosom with both hands and making sucking noises with his mouth. She unbuttoned her shirt and let one of her breasts plop out. The baby grabbed it and put it in his mouth. PJ wasn't used to seeing women's breasts. He had a hard time keeping his eyes looking the other way.

"You got no particular reason to give credence to what I is about to tell you," the man went on, popping a chocolate drop in his mouth. "But it's the truth. And Junior will know I speak with veracity."

Glory saw that PJ was watching her and the baby. Embarrassed, he looked away. But she didn't, and when he glanced back again her eyes were there to catch and hold his. She smiled, and he couldn't keep from smiling too. It was all right.

"Junior here knows my Laveria. She our onliest daughter. Married now; living in Jackson. Now she grown, she don't come to the River no more. But Misses Light and me been here in this very place every 'teenth since befo' Junior was born. The reason has to do with the grandfather of these two here." He looked at Glory and Junior as if they were both his own pride and joy.

Junior sat cross-legged on the edge of the blanket. His arms, supple and strong in a clean white shirt, lay at rest on his legs. The sun was in his eyes, but he didn't seem to notice. He waited for what the Reverend had to say as if he already knew.

"You know, PJ, among the colored, happiness is the family. The big families is the happy families. Mens and womens that gets married and don't got no children is poor indeed."

"Misses Light and me, we was that a way," he explained. "We took it to the Lord. Prayed on it. We took it to the hospitals. She had the tests. I had the tests. They say they don't see nothin' wrong. Still, no little one was a comin'."

"My Daddy, you know he was raised up over here jes south of Theodosa, he was visitin'. He notice how it grieve us. 'Son, he tole me, there is more ways than white folks ways.' And he caused us to seek counsel with Junior's grandfather."

"Misses Light and me, we come over here and met up with Mr. Dunfee. You understand he don't hear none and he don't talk none, but he understood everything."

"The short of it was, a divination was carried out and we came to know there was somebody holdin' anger against my wife. 'That anger has to be killed off,' he say. Of course, Mr. Dunfee he don't speak, but that was what he was saying."

Glory took the baby off the one breast and put him on the other one. PJ thought those breasts were the most beautiful things he had ever seen in his life.

"Three thangs was needed," Reverend Light said. "A yard of calico, a bottle of liquor spirits and a live chicken. And we come off to this here place, right here, because it needs a river to work."

The Reverend was still on his knees explaining. "The calico was tied 'round my wife at the middle. The chicken was situated on her head and she has to hold it with both hands. Mr. Dunfee he walk up and down and my wife she walk up and down. Mr. Dunfee he commence to talkin' in a language that was his own, and he was pourin' liquor on the ground.

My wife she was holding on to keep that chicken from flyin' off. Mr. Dunfee commence to dance and to call out in that old language. He pour some more liquor on the ground and put some over in the River."

"Of a sudden, the chicken let out its droppin's. They come down all over her. And when the woman puts dat chicken down, it was a dead chicken. Mr. Dunfee, he take it and throw it in de river. It warn't too long after that, the woman she got the mornin' sickness and in nine months more, Laveria, our blessed child, was born."

"You don't believe that?" The Reverend Light was looking at PJ as if it really did matter that he believed him.

PJ didn't know how to answer.

Reverend Light turned to Lee Junior. "You believe that." Lee Junior didn't answer either, but he sat looking at the Reverend as if it seemed to make sense.

When everybody saw that Mr. Dunfee could step on his shadow in the midday sun, they knew it was time to eat. And there was lots of food and they all ate a lot, except for PJ who couldn't get past the picture of Mrs. Light with a chicken on her head. Every time he saw her take a bite of sweet potato pie, his very favorite, he kept thinking of the chicken droppings running through her hair, coming off onto her pretty flowered dress.

The fire was out. Mr. Dunfee was wrapping pieces of goat meat in newspapers and giving everybody some to take home.

"This here's a tender piece," Nettie told PJ. "Miss Belle will like this," she said, handing him a small package. "I thanks you for what you done."

She then showed him a slightly larger package. "And this here one, I'm a'goin' to take it right over to Mr. Sapp myself," she said.

By mid-afternoon, they had loaded everything back into

the truck. In caravan, they all drove over to find the old Negro cemetery. The place was now fenced off by the lumber company. The families got out and picked their way through briars and low brush for about a half a mile struggling to make their way through the Cutover where the big longleaf pines once stood.

PJ tried to imagine the time before the pines were cut, when the woods were open, and there were no brambles. He had heard that early settlers in wagons could travel for days under the canopy of the pines on a nearly endless meadow of grass.

The Cherokee, the Shawnee and the Alabama Coushatta Indians had kept the entire coastal plain open from Southern Virginia to East Texas by setting fire to the wiregrass that grew up in the understory. Longleaf pines thrived on fire, and the tender plants that regrew beneath them attracted the wildlife the Indians needed to survive there for a thousand years or more.

But now, since the lumber companies had taken the old forest down, what remained was just an endless tangle of brush and briers coming up around the stumps, fighting for every little bit of sunlight alongside the new growth of over-crowded loblolly pines and sweet gum trees.

It was not easy finding where the old cemetery was. A big holly, some cedars and a few crepe myrtles still marked the burial ground. The ancient oaks had been cut by loggers, probably for no more than a few railroad ties. What was left were some gnarled limbs big as tree trunks felled across the wrought-iron fence.

The gravestones, some of them no more than creek stones or big pieces of petrified wood, were all in disarray. The families, looking for familiar markers, pulled at the weeds and tried to put things back. It didn't help much. They were too late.

The Reverend called people over to see a flat stone onto which the word SAMBO had been etched.

"Y'all know the story of Little Black Sambo," he said. "But what almost nobody but us knows is that Sambo is not just the name of a little boy. Sambo is a place we all must remember. You get yourself a map of the world. Sambo was – and still is – the name of a village on the west coast of Africa. And dats where we from. And here we are."

By dusk dark, PJ had the truck parked back at the gin shop and was walking home. In his hand, he carried a mess of goat meat barbeque wrapped in newspaper. Normally, he would have been running, but on this evening he was not. He was thinking, and not yet ready for the day to end.

What he had the hardest time comprehending was that a whole village of people from a place called Sambo were brought to America, some of them now dead and buried right here in the great forest Cutover of Theodosa County. And that no one but him and these folks who were celebrating their emancipation from slavery had any idea where the people from Sambo had ended up.

A New Breed of Cattle

Since the Juneteenth celebration, the old Cutover between the Sandy Prairie and the Theodosa River began to have the same kind of attraction over PJ that a magnet has over a steel ball bearing.

He couldn't explain exactly why. The more he learned about the place, the more he wanted to know what it was and why it was there. The families that resided in and around the Cutover became to him very much like characters in a good mystery story. Only, these people were alive, and he could go visit them and ask them questions.

PJ had been taking longer runs down the River road looking for landmarks, both natural and man-made. He explored places where he could move inward toward the heart of the thicket.

He revisited the lost Negro cemetery on his own and made memory notes of the place and took the time to do some on-site sketches. In digging around there, he found a couple of marbles and the head of a small ceramic doll. These he put into his leather backpack to add to his local artifacts collection, which he kept in a box on a shelf on his side of the bedroom.

At the Crossroads store, an old logger told PJ where he might locate the corridors of the former narrow-gauge railroad the lumber companies had laid through the forest. The man drew PJ a crude map on the back of a grocery sack, showing how the PP&G tracks ran mostly east to west parallel to the River.

In those days, the man told him with a laugh, "It was officially the PP&G, but everybody called that old locomotive the Push Pull and Grunt." Going by the crude map, PJ found some old abutments where the railroad had crossed over creeks.

PJ also explored the cavities left by the dynamite crews that had moved into the Cutover during wartime to blast the longleaf pine stumps out of the ground. The old logger had described to him how during the War giant dozers and lifting equipment hoisted the turpentine-saturated roots into trucks, hauling the fatwood to gum mills out of state.

PJ had been surprised to hear the man say, "In sandy soil, the taproots of the longleaf can grow as deep as the trees are tall." In looking at those bombed-out holes and the rich-litered pine scattered around, PJ could see the truth in what the old man had told him.

Now, other changes were coming to the Cutover. Two weeks after the Juneteenth celebration, PJ learned that Mr. Sapp was having a large piece of that Cutover cleared with the idea of raising cattle there.

PJ got this news from his neighbor Joe Truehaw, a former agriculture teacher who had come to the Prairie some three years earlier. Joe had bought the old Clegg farm, which was just about a mile down the road from where PJ lived.

PJ knew the place well. He wasn't even nine years old when he discovered the big pear tree behind the Clegg house. It produced the sweetest pears he had ever tasted. Nobody had cared for that farm for a long time. The fences were down and the pastures had grown up in grass burrs and crawfish mounds. The big barn on the Clegg place had burned just before Joe and his daughter Joey Lou arrived on the Prairie.

The Truehaws worked first on making the house livable. Then, Joey Lou, who was 14 when they arrived, started getting the fields ready to plant peanuts and corn. She learned to drive a tractor in her first year while cutting and raking hay for neighbor Pootie Wilson, and he then loaned her the use of his tractor and sod buster for breaking up the hardpan ground on her own place.

Meanwhile, her dad had set to work acquiring the lumber needed to build a new corncrib. Joe Truehaw soon realized, however, that marauding hogs coming up out of the Cutover meant that rebuilding fences had to be the higher priority.

That was when he first enlisted PJ to help him start pulling down those old barbwire fences. He wanted to start over with good post and strong hog wire.

Now, Joey Lou was 17 years old. Since her father spent so much time helping Mr. Sapp, it had fallen to her to do the farming part by herself. That was just fine with her. It didn't take long for her to show people that she could handle it like a man.

In the beginning, neighbors were patient and even helpful toward the Truehaws, considering that the Clegg place was in such disrepair. Now, three years later, the word going around was that the father was too much of a perfectionist, which explained why he could never finish anything. And there was PJ still helping him build fence.

The source of many of those hurtful opinions, PJ came to learn, traced to the store manager, Bee Beeman. He thought it mean-spirited of him. Why would he go out of his way to put the man down?

For himself, PJ had concluded that Joe Truehaw was one of a handful of people on the Prairie who ought to be addressed as "Mr." These people included Mr. Sapp, his landlord, Mr. Dromgould, his school principal, and Mr. Beeman, himself.

Not that Joe Truehaw expected the title. Joe specifically asked PJ not to call him Mr.

Still, PJ felt the man deserved that show of respect in public because he was a college graduate in soils engineering, he had taught high school before he came to Theodosa County, and he was a reader of books and magazines.

Joe Truehaw cared about things that hardly anybody else paid attention to, like the need to install terraces to help prevent soil erosion in cotton and peanut fields. He spoke to the need for Prairie farmers to diversify their crops to be more competitive in the global market, which nobody but Joe — and maybe Mr. Sapp - knew anything about. He also worried about the plight of the American Indians, especially those who lived just across the River on a government-established reservation.

When helping Joe Truehaw build fence, PJ already knew that there was a special way he wanted it done. In digging post holes, he expected PJ to be careful to keep to the straight line that Joe had stretched on his side of the road, including the line that went down into lower spots and eventually crossed the creek. He also knew that each post should be set at least 14-inches deep, and that the tallest post should be the ones installed at lowest ground levels.

It was then that PJ learned about the Brahma cattle, and he was surprised. "I didn't know Mr. Sapp had any interest in raising cows?" PJ prided himself in knowing about whatever was happening around the Cutover.

"Cyrus doesn't want to talk much about it." Joe told him. He was marking where each hole should be dug, precisely at twelve feet apart. "Our Mr. Sapp would just as soon not spread the word until we can figure out whether this project is going to work, or not."

Without a hat, Joe had to keep pushing his hair back out of his eyes. He was saying, "But I guess people will find out soon enough. We have already taken the first steps to bring into our region a new breed of cattle we've never had here before. Have you ever heard of Brahmas?"

"No, Sir, I haven't." PJ said, not stopping his good working rhythm. "But, I would like to hear about that."

Ahead of him, Joe was pulling out honeysuckle vines from the old fencerow. He started in explaining that Mr. Sapp had contracted with one of the big equipment operators up at Theodosa to clear a piece of bottom land that he had purchased from the lumber companies. "That ground is now seeded in a pasture grass, and is already coming up."

"And, once the land was cleared and seeded," Joe Truehaw told him, "Mr. Sapp hired a work crew to come and build him a big two-story barn. That barn is up now. It has a very impressive lot all around it with a high board fence made of 2X6 oak boards."

Joe had drug the honeysuckle vines he was digging out over to the side, making a burn pile. He told PJ, "All the big hardwood timbers along the creeks down there were already stripped out. There's hardly a tree left that is big enough to cut into lumber. I think that is a real shame. But that new oil road, FM 2121, has made it a lot easier to get back there."

"The idea for raising Brahma cattle," Joe explained, "came from an article in the *Farmer Stockman* about a new breed developed in South Texas during the Depression. I showed it to Mr. Sapp, and he got interested in it."

Joe went and got post from the wagon and helped PJ set them in the holes he had dug. He continued with his story from the magazine. "What happened was the ranchers from Texas had imported some Brahma-type cows from India and bred them to some big Brazilian bulls. Their offspring tended to also be big and hearty, and they took the heat well. Because of their size, they made good beef producers."

Joe was again pushing his hair out of his eyes. "That article said the Brahma would graze on rough browse, bushes and small trees as well as grass. They could survive in drought conditions and still bring top dollar at the slaughterhouse. Cyrus decided to try it, and asked me to help him."

In July 1950, two big loads of Brahma cows, plus two bulls, arrived to start the breeding program. PJ was not the only one in Theodosa County who had never seen an animal like this. The Brahmas released onto the newly fenced pasture on FM 2121 turned out to be something of a circus curiosity. Sunday afternoons became popular times for local folks to drive over and take a look.

PJ too would climb up on the big gates just outside the lot to study them. These were very large animals. The females were tall and slender, mostly white with black shading. When on alert, they stood up straight, snapping their heads upward to show off their high horns. The two bulls, noticeably heavier and more muscular, each sported an abnormally big hump on its shoulders right behind its head.

From the perspective of the fence, PJ examined the Brahmas with considerable interest and admiration. Observing the ease with which the two bulls made their way from cow to cow, he came to the opinion that only two bulls would be sufficient for servicing that large herd. Mr. Beeman had specifically asked about that.

In addition to being manager of the store at the Crossroads, it was widely known that Mr. Beeman was the self-appointed collector and broadcaster of any and all local news. The fact that he wasn't the first to learn about "a new Brahma Breeding Station going in on the far West side of the Cutover" put him in a difficult position.

He clearly needed to be first with any new information. But Cyrus Sapp, the owner of the store, hadn't bothered to tell him anything at all about his latest venture. He had only confided in Joe Truehaw. This was an obvious embarrassment to Mr. Beeman.

The store manager figured out early on that Joe Truehaw must be the one behind this whole development, but there was no way he was going to come right out and ask him about it. So, he turned to PJ.

That's how it was that a 14-year-old became the principal source of information about Brahma cattle in Theodosa County. A case in point, Mr. Beeman, the store manager, was publicly crediting PJ for his on-site observation that "the two male Brahmas weren't spending much time eating grass."

At first, it appeared that the Brahma wonder cow might have all the fine qualities that the magazine said about them. For PJ, watching them graze in the newly planted pastures and seeing them lie in the shade of the few trees left along the creek was like a movie in Technicolor at the Theodosa picture show. The sun was shining, the cows were white, the grass was green, the skies were blue; they seemed to have made themselves right at home.

PJ climbed up the gnarled limbs of an old live oak, pulled out his sketching pencils and made drawings of Brahmas in different poses. He also made notes on Brahma behavior.

Not all of what PJ observed was encouraging news for the Brahma managers: Truehaw and Sapp. For one thing, he thought that the two of them may have been overly optimistic about how manageable this breed of cattle would be. From watching them, he knew right away that these were not a bunch of milk cows. These Brahmas had a wild streak.

The magazine Mr. Sapp had read said that the Brahma cows were known to do well in the wild brushy outback of South Texas. But the literature failed to mention that a Brahma will resist being shut up in any kind of pen. What PJ concluded, and told Mr. Beeman, was that these animals didn't have even a basic understanding of the purpose of a fence or a barn.

From what PJ could see, human beings were totally irrelevant to Brahma cattle. He had written in his own notes: "Every time Mr. Sapp's cowboys try to herd them into the barn, they just split up and run in every direction." He also wrote, "Last night, some of the cattle got spooked for some reason or another and broke right through Mr. Sapp's new fence - and it is a barbed wire fence! About a dozen Brahmas are now out in the road, headed no telling where."

But it didn't take PJ very long to also realize that the opinions he was relaying to Mr. Bee about Brahma behavior, the store manager was sharing as fact with everybody else. And it was not unknown for him to reframe and embellish what PJ shared with him. An example of this was Mr. Bee's conclusion that these "Brahmas aren't amenable to domestication."

Joe Truehaw soon realized he had a bigger challenge than he expected. He was not only advising Mr. Sapp on how to turn the Brahma into a source of store-bought beef, he was having to help him figure out how to keep these large animals on Sapp property.

It was probably because of this that Cyrus Sapp, with Joe Truehaw's recommendation, hired PJ to report on any loose Brahmas spotted about the Prairie, so they could send their rapidly growing team of cowboys out to round them up. Mr. Sapp proposed to pay PJ two dollars a week just to let him know when there might be a problem with his cows or his fences.

Another matter that Mr. Sapp found not at all easy to solve was what to do when a Brahma got sick. This problem arose when some of his cattle became infested with screwworms.

PJ was helping out at the Breeding Station when Joe Truehaw explained about the screwworm. Mr. Sapp was there. One of Ralph Sonora's men had roped and tied up a calf they wanted Mr. Sapp to look at.

Joe was saying "We are finding the eggs of these screwworm flies in the naval canals in some of our newborn calves. But the screwworm fly can deposit its eggs in the wound of any injured animal. We have already doctored a case of a momma cow that got tangled up in one of our barbed wire fences. These flies were attracted to the cow and laid their eggs in an open cut in her underbelly."

Joe told them that screwworm outbreaks usually happen in the tropics where the weather isn't cold enough to kill them off, but he explained that these flies have now migrated far enough north to infect our cattle here. He wasn't sure but thought, "maybe we imported them with this herd."

"Screwworm sores are easy enough to treat with a salve, if you can capture the animal to doctor it," Joe said as he pushed his hair back out of his eyes.

"What salve would that be?" Cyrus Sapp wondered.

"I think we can pretty easily make an arsenic mix with turpentine cooked out of longleaf pine knots from right around here," Joe told him.

"But we'll have to catch and hold the animal down to apply it, won't we?" Mr. Sapp worried.

"Well, yes, the wound has to be cut open and the grubs dug out. If you can manage to hold that cow down, one person can do that with a sharp pocket knife," Joe agreed. "Then the sore has to be swabbed inside and out."

"I know Ralph's boys can rope and tie up calves," Cyrus said, "and sometimes they will be able to catch and hold grown animals. But that's going to be pretty hard for them to do out in the thick brush of the Cutover."

Listening to this, PJ thought to himself, "These Brahmas may seem nice and calm at first – but they could be really dangerous in a tight spot."

The Sapp and Truehaw solution to the screwworm infestation had two parts to it. PJ admired the efficiency of both. One was the construction of a dipping vat just outside the new lot on FM 2121, and the other was the fabrication of a squeeze chute that would funnel the cattle into it.

Joe Truehaw had helped design and build each of these

structures. Together, they consisted of a concrete trough about 25 feet long, six-to-seven feet deep and three feet wide that was filled with an arsenic water solution. The trough was positioned at the convergence of two long and widely spaced fences so that drivers on horses could press small herds of cows and calves into it, forcing the livestock down into the liquid solution one by one.

This approach had the advantage of providing a preventive doctoring of every part of each animal's body below the head. For the cows and calves already infected by the screwworm fly, the Brahma handlers devised a way, that when the livestock came up out of the dipping solution, they could switch a gate to hold those animals in a squeeze chute for further inspection and doctoring.

This mechanical device provided a whole-body lock that prevented the animal from hooking or kicking or slamming its weight around, for medication or dehorning or branding. While the round-up crew were pushing these cattle through, the Brahma Breeding Station people intended to burn a large BBS mark onto the left shank of each cow and calf.

In the notebook that PJ carried in his backpack, he made pencil notes and drew illustrated designs for himself showing how the dipping vat and squeeze chute were set up. He thought the way they worked together was such a fine piece of engineering that he should make a record of it. Now, Mr. Sapp should be able to doctor his Brahmas without anybody losing an arm or an eye.

Now that the dipping vat and squeeze chute were in place, the next question was--how to get them to enter the lot?

The "gentle-them-down" plan, which the two managers worked out and implemented over the course of several weeks, did appear to work for a while. The strategy was to leave the gate to the barn lot always open and entice the cattle in with a plentiful supply of food and water.

The men assigned to the job put loose hay every day in the racks inside the barn, and kept a mixture of silage, cottonseed meal and salt available in the troughs. The cows were free to come in, to feed at will and to go out whenever they liked.

Some of the Brahmas and a number of rogue hogs must have

68

liked this arrangement, since the feed in the barn was eaten every day and the water tank had to be refilled. The problem was that when any human being showed up, the animals promptly ran out of the barn. That person could stay there all day but no cows would enter when people were present. The two bulls came in and went out as they pleased. The more wary females and their calves stayed outside.

Mr. Sapp and Joe Truehaw developed a fallback plan that called on PJ's assistance. With his mother Belle's permission, PJ agreed to run over to FM 2121 after dark and shut the gate on the Brahmas when they were all inside.

The first time he went was around 8 PM, but there were no cows to be seen, inside the barn lot or out. He waited a few days and went at 10 pm. Some were grazing outside and a few were inside, but when they heard PJ coming, they all stormed out before he was even near to the gate.

Negotiations with his mother led to PJ going at midnight. This time, by approaching the BBS barn more cautiously, PJ got close enough to recognize that there were a substantial number of cows in the lot.

Although the moon was mostly hiding behind clouds, he could make out that the herd had stationed a sentinel just outside the gate. PJ lay face-down in the grass and waited. The big high-horned Brahma cow that stood in silhouette against the night sky eventually went inside, but another came out to take her place.

PJ began to crawl on his belly in the direction of the gate. His thought was to get close enough to make a run for it and shut the gate before many of them could escape.

It didn't work out that way. The second sentinel saw him. She must have been curious about what was crawling on the ground, because she slowly walked to within ten feet of where PJ lay in the grass. Towering over him, the cow lowered her head and sniffed twice, but he held his prone position and did not move.

He was soon aware of movement from other directions, and came to the scary realization that these tall animals were forming a circle around him. He couldn't tell how many there were, but he did not doubt they all were there because of him.

One cow eventually broke the circle and stepped forward. She moved directly above him and lowered her head, touching her cold wet nose to his ear. He tried with all his might not to move, but when she gave a wet lick of her rough tongue cross his face, he couldn't take it anymore. "Yuuuck!" he exclaimed. And the Brahmas all broke and ran away.

By the time PJ got to his feet, the cows had disappeared into the dark night. He left the barn gate wide open as it was before he came. There was nothing more to do.

For years, PJ had stopped by the store almost every weekday, plus Saturdays, to be there when his mother got dropped off from work. He helped out with little jobs Mr. Bee always had for him to do.

It just seemed quite natural for him to share with Mr. Beeman what he was up to about the Prairie and down into the Cutover, including his frustration about those animals on FM 2121. Mr. Beeman was a sympathetic listener.

It was perhaps not surprising that PJ often figured into the stories the store manager reported to his customers. This young man was seeing things nearly every day that Mr. Beeman needed to know about. Incidents or activity related to this rare breed of cattle were among the topics of current and continuing interest.

The problem for Mr. Beeman was that the owner of these Brahmas was his boss, and Mr. Sapp wasn't saying much. The emerging problem for PJ was that his lifelong friend at the store tended to turn anything he said into community gossip.

On Thursday afternoon, while PJ was waiting for his mother Belle, he was helping Mr. Beeman and John, the ice delivery-man from town, unload 50-pound blocks of clear ice from the man's truck. PJ's task was to slide the ice down a homemade ramp into the sawdust-insulated shed at the front of the Crossroads store.

Mr. Beeman was on the ground using ice tongs to lift and stack the blocks of ice into the ice house. As both John and PJ could see, the store manager was not in physical condition to be doing such heavy lifting, and he paused every few minutes to catch his breath. But Mr. Bee couldn't help trying to talk.

He picked up an earlier conversation he and his friend John

had apparently been having about Mr. Sapp's new project down on FM 2121. "It looks like Joe Truehaw's dipping vat idea isn't going to work," he said as he caught his breath. "How can it, when they are never going to catch and hold those Brahma cattle in any kind of a pen?"

Mr. Beeman spoke directly to PJ, who stood between the two of them. "Isn't that what you figure, PJ? Then the store manager looked around, as if the three of them might be overheard. "Don't y'all tell Mr. Sapp I said that. All right?"

When PJ also looked up to see whether Mr. Sapp might actually be somewhere near-by, the store manager must have realized that he was putting PJ in an awkward position. Mr. Beeman stepped forward and put his hand on PJ's shoulder. "I'm sorry, Son. I shouldn't have said that. I know Mr. Sapp is proud of you, and I am too."

In PJ's mind, he was just trying to keep the news straight, and up-to-date. He wasn't drawing conclusions. He had his own opinion, of course, about whether the new dipping vat was going to work, or not. But he certainly wouldn't himself say such a thing to Mr. Sapp. He didn't know near enough to have an informed opinion about that.

Apparently, because he saw the boy's reaction, Mr. Beeman then stepped forward to put his hand on PJ's shoulder. He said, "PJ, I know you are now in the employ of Mr. Sapp. You don't have to answer that question."

This turn of events had surprised PJ, but he took it as a gesture of recognition, from someone who knew him well, that he was no longer just a boy. He was now old enough to be seen as a man, and to be treated as a man.

As if to reinforce the thought, the store manager looked at the iceman and said something that was quite surprising to PJ. "John, I want you to mark my words. This young man will grow up to be a newspaper man or radio reporter someday." Mr. Beeman pointed to PJ's backpack that was lying in the grass at the edge of the ice house, "Sandy Prairie's own Peyton Jackson Purdee will be the first with the words and the pictures to illustrate all our stories, whatever they are."

What an amazing idea! PJ thought. Might that really be true?

Even if it wasn't, it did please him to receive such praise from Mr. Bee. He wondered if these words came from the store manager because he knew PJ did not have a father to be proud of him and he was obliged to say things like that?

It was Mr. Beeman who changed the subject. He said to John, "Have I told you before that our PJ here was born breech?"

"No, Bee, I don't think I know what 'born breech' means."

"It means that his mother Belle delivered him feet first."

Mr. Bee saw the opening to tell more about the story. "As you know, this boy's father was off at war, and his mother was staying here on the Prairie with her in-laws, Claire Ruth and Snappy P. Purdee. So I was the one who drove over to get Nettie Johnson, the colored mid-wife, to come help the boy get born."

"And when Belle still couldn't deliver, I was the one who called Dr. Peyton Jackson to come in from town to get the job done. I am told that this boy is one of the few who ever survive coming feet-first into the world. I know for a fact that young PJ here almost didn't make it."

Both the ice man and PJ were just standing and waiting. Mr. Beeman finally signaled for more ice to come down but went right on talking. "John, you grew up in Theodosa. You knew this boy's father, Rayford Purdee? Our star basketball player at the high school, who got killed in the war? And his mother, Belle Carr, the coach's daughter?

"Well, yes. I didn't know him personally, but I knew about him," John replied. He paused and spoke directly to PJ, "Son, I am really sorry for your loss."

But Mr. Beeman went on, "Then, John, I would expect you remember about that home basketball game when the girls team played our boys team – the year Theodosa High was State Champion? PJ's mother and daddy were on opposite sides in that game - and the girls won!"

"I never saw that game," John admitted, "but of course I heard about it. Old folks like us are still wondering why that game turned out the way it did."

The iceman held onto an ice block he was about to pass on to PJ. "Boy, help me be clear about something I have been wondering about. Your other grandfather was Jim Carr, who was basketball coach at Theodosa High? Do I have that right?"

"Yes, Sir, that's what I was told. But I never met him." PJ caught the block and passed it on to Mr. Beeman, who hooked his ice tongs into it and pulled it into the icehouse. As PJ turned to catch the next one, the iceman looked at him directly.

"Well, PJ, let me tell you something you may not yet know about. I was watching the sports news on my TV last night, and I saw that Jim Carr just signed on as head basketball coach at the University of Florida in Gainesville."

"Jim Carr?" Mr. Beeman whistled in amazement. "My goodness gracious. Is that right, John?"

PJ looked at the man in amazement.

"I know y'all don't get the TV signal down here. Did you by chance happen to know about that?"

PJ didn't say anything. His mind was fixed on the pressing present reality that his mother would be arriving on the Prairie within the next hour. Indeed, if it was true, he thought it would be very likely that she would have also heard this news. . . . And there was that other thing to consider: He also knew that there was no way of knowing what frame of mind she might be in.

PJ's Pap

"Chesterfields," PJ said.

"Chesterfields." Mr. Beeman repeated, as if trying to decide whether that would be acceptable or not.

"Yes sir."

Mr. Beeman kept all cigarettes for sale in a tall glass case beside the cash register. Cigarettes ranked among the store's precious small goods like snuff, chewing tobacco, wind-up alarm clocks and K-bar knives. They were up front on display, and not left out on a shelf, just to make sure the proprietor of the store was the only one who could get at them.

Mr. Beeman studied PJ for a moment through his bushy red eyebrows, then turned and opened the case. He took the white and yellow packet of cigarettes from its larger carton and set the pack upright on the counter, but continued to hold it between his thumb and forefinger as if undecided.

PJ's six nickels were already lined up in a row on the counter.

"You think it's the right thing to do, PJ?"

"No sir."

"I don't either," Mr. Beeman said. A grey tabby hopped up onto the counter. It stepped across the change and rubbed against the bulging softness of Mr. Beeman's stomach. Neither of them took notice of the cat.

A car honked at the gas pumps out front. Mr. Beeman let go of the Chesterfields and quickly scooped the change from the counter. These he dropped into the nickel drawer of the cash register.

PJ picked up the small package and deftly slid it into an upper pocket of his overalls. He followed the store manager out the door and down the three wide steps that led out to the gas pumps and the Crossroads.

It was mid-morning, but the day was already hot. PJ left the store on foot, paced at a fast trot, not at a full run but fast enough to work up a sweat. He could feel the heat in the sand on the balls of his bare feet. Heat waves were spreading out across neighboring fields on either side of the road, all of them already plowed and harrowed, most were planted and showing crops.

He guessed he had run maybe a hundred times the two-something miles between the store at the Crossroads and the Purdee farm where his grandparents lived. It was way more times than that if you counted the trips he took on foot running to and from the school, the church and the cotton gin.

PJ knew almost everybody who lived and worked on the Prairie and he knew many among the Cutover homesteads that were spread out between the River and the Prairie. He prided himself on that. It was true that people said of him, "PJ comes over to help out" and "He will just show up anytime you might need him." He didn't mind what they said, because that is what he enjoyed doing.

As he ran on that morning, he tried to remember when he first became a runner. When he first started picking up his pace a little, and then more and more, it was just a quicker way to get from the place he was to the places he wanted to go.

When it might take longer to go by the road, he would just climb the fence and cut across the fields, often following the edges of streams.

Running in the woods was his specialty. Dodging trees and stumps and leaping into dry creek beds without knowing exactly where he would land was the most fun of all.

At the picture show in Theodosa, PJ had seen a war movie about Iwo Jima. The American soldiers in the movie had to make a decision about how to take out some Japs that were in a foxhole up ahead. A young soldier volunteered for this duty and took off all his heavy equipment, including his steel helmet. With his buddies' help, he hung four hand grenades on his belt and carried one in each hand.

They patted him on the back and he took off running fast.

The enemy saw him coming toward them through the woods

and started firing. The soldier was dodging machine gun bullets all the way.

He pulled the pin on the first grenade as he ran and threw it in the direction of the foxhole up ahead. It made a big explosion. The grenade had fallen short but all the sand and smoke in the air had given him enough cover to get in closer as he ran forward.

His second grenade hit its mark and took out the Japs and blew up their machine gun nest.

Talking with his brother Roy later about that scene in the movie, the one thing he couldn't understand was why that soldier would keep his boots on if he was needing to run fast and dodge bullets. Surely, that young soldier must have known how much faster and quicker he would have been if he were running barefooted.

PJ's grandpap was sitting on the shady ground out by the tractor shed, his back up against the big post oak. He had positioned himself so he could spot the boy coming down the road from the store. He had his hand stuck out when PJ came trotting up to where he sat waiting.

The smile on his grandfather's face turned to almost childlike anticipation when the boy pulled the package of Chesterfield cigarettes from the bib of his overalls and handed them over to him.

PJ squatted in the sand in front of his pap and watched the man he loved more than anyone in the world tear open the package and exhaust himself trying to shake out a single cigarette. In his impatience, he dumped its entire contents out into his lap, long white cigarettes spilling over onto the dirt around him.

With a cigarette in his mouth he began to fumble with both hands to get a match from his shirt pocket and strike it with his thumbnail. When the phosphor finally flared and he touched its flame to the cigarette, he bit down on it and made a loud sucking sound, drawing air deep into his lungs.

Suppressing a cough, he held the smoke for almost a full minute until it began to escape of its own force out of his flared nose and trembling mouth.

When he finally released his breath he still didn't open his mouth. He just parted his lips to let a great woosh of smoke come rushing through the yellow teeth that gripped his fiery cigarette. He drew in on the cigarette again, and then again.

Pinching the white stalk of tobacco between his thumb and forefinger, he finally took it out and looked at it, grinning and shaking his head. "PJ," he whispered, as if he were experiencing extraordinary pleasure in his great pain, "if there's any thang that is better than pussy, this is it."

PJ's grandpap, "Snappy P" Purdee, was dying of lung cancer. He couldn't half breathe because he only had half a lung left.

"Too many years of breathing in exhaust fumes, peanut dust and cotton fiber," Dr. Peyton Jackson had said. "That and smoking a pack of Chesterfields every day."

With a collapsed lung and spitting blood, he hadn't the strength of a nursing baby. He couldn't walk more than ten steps without having to stop to catch his breath; but for Snappy P, ten wobbly steps were enough to get himself out of the house, and ten more were enough to be at the entrance to the tractor shed.

On good days, by himself, he could get his old Allis-Chalmers model B tractor started and headed in the direction of the field, but there was really nothing out there for him to do but drive to the back of the field, come back, and do it again.

"Stubborn as a mule." That's what Grandee told him to his face. And that's the way she referred to him when Belle, her daughter-in-law, inquired about how he was doing. "He doesn't hear a thing I say." Ever since his pap first got real sick six months earlier, Granny Purdee had tried to keep his grandfather on a short leash. It wasn't easy.

Grandee had laid down the law with the neighbors as well as the family. "You are not to help him put those cultivators on that tractor, no matter what he says or does," she told them.

"I can't have him out there plowing up my cotton."

The result was that Pap just drove his tractor around the perimeter of the field until he ran out of gas or ended up stalled in the fencerow. Gran would send PJ and Lee Junior to go get him and bring him back to the house.

People from all over knew Snappy Purdee. He had been the

morning and afternoon bus driver through several generations of school children.

In the middle of most days, when he could be found working as a mechanic at the gin shop, he was willing to drop everything, get into his old Studebaker pickup with the toolbox in back and come fix whatever needed to be repaired, be it a grandmother clock, a baby's high chair or pieces of equipment that were as big as a bulldozer.

Excepting maybe for the preacher, Prairie people went out of their way to be around Snappy P. His grandson PJ had been trying to figure exactly why for a long time.

Maybe it was because his Pap remembered people's names or because he saved up off-color jokes and stories to tell.

Snappy P used to play the mandolin, harmonica and jew's harp at school and Prairie events. He was able to play just about any tune someone wanted to hear. Those were the good days.

Boys hung around him because he would talk to them about things adults wouldn't admit to. From their Pap, Roy and PJ got a straight answer about the meaning of what church people called Original Sin.

On a trip when he had arranged for the boys to go with him to the State Prison Rodeo, their grandfather explained why it was most people thought sex was sinful. There were two ideas he wanted to get across as a lesson for the boys to remember.

One was: "You absolutely must not under any circumstances get any girl pregnant." And the other one was: "You take responsibility if you make a mistake."

Their pap told them, "Boys, you can be a stray tomcat going from barn to barn in the dark of the night, but I can tell you there ain't no such thing as free love. It all has to be paid for one way or another, if not by you, by somebody else."

He would be very specific. "You boys know how you make girls pregnant. If you are going to take that chance, you better think about getting yourself a rubber. Let me tell you straight: you do not want to make babies until you are ready to be a father to them."

He talked about a "social contract" that everybody knows is

the right thing to do, but not everybody keeps. It had to do with taking personal responsibility. "You don't bring harm to nobody if you can help it. When it comes to having sex with a woman, you better be protected or you better be ready to raise a child."

"The preacher, he will tell you it's a sin to be with a woman unless you are married to her. And maybe it is. It certainly can be because it can make a real mess. But I am telling you boys that just getting a hard on is not a sin, and jacking off is not a sin. You should do it in private but let me say what nobody else around here is going to tell you: it is all just a natural part of growing up and becoming a man. It is not a sin."

On a trip the three of them had taken to the State Prison Rodeo, their grandfather told them some stories about when he was young. "I was seein' a long-legged girl that lived over at the Pharris place," he said. "We were meetin' at night after her family was asleep."

"One night I couldn't wait to get some of that and went over there a little early. The light was still on, so I crawled up beside the house and waited. Before long, her daddy came out on the porch to take a leak. Well he just pissed right down on top of my head, went all down my neck and into my shirt. I never knew if he saw me or not."

"Anyway, I didn't stay around to see that girl that night. What her father did kind of dampened my ardor."

"I tell you about this because I am not proud of what I was doing. I hope you boys will have the patience and the good sense to wait until the right lady comes along for you.

"They say that you can wear it out," Pap once told them, speaking from a grandfather's perspective, "that it's like a typewriter. When the ribbon is fresh and new, it prints black. But the more you use it, the dimmer and dimmer it gets until there's nothing a'tall.

"I haven't seen that," he said. "I know when you're young, that snake is up in a flash raring to take on the first Eve that shows up in your garden. Later on, I guess it takes more than a look, but I don't ever see you wearing it out. It's just one of man's basic pleasures. It's the way we are made."

His grandfather's illness showed up early that spring. He was so slowed down he wasn't able to get his Allis-Chalmers started so he could back his old peanut thresher out of the tractor shed. He sent PJ to ask Lee Junior if he would bring his John Deere over and help pull the big machine out under the post oak.

He was wanting to get it ready for fall peanut harvest. Neither Lee Junior or PJ understood at the time why Pap was getting equipment ready three months earlier than it would be needed.

Pap's prized threshing machine may have been the last one left in the county to do custom work one field at a time. Cars driving by on the road would stop to see what was making such a big cloud of dust. Snappy P's thresher was shaking the soil off the late summer peanuts, separating the nuts from the roots, leaving behind piles of dried roots and vines. At the end of the day, fifty-pound bags of raw peanuts would be stacked up in each of the fields he worked in.

The peanut thresher was a huge wood and tin frame with steel wheels that at a distance looked like a bright red box of fireplace matches sitting on edge, standing higher than two men tall. Even though it was covered with dust at the end of the season, by the time of next year's harvest, Snappy's machine was greased and oiled inside, and cleaned up and polished on the outside.

Neither PJ or Lee Junior could see how that was going to happen this year. The old man was hardly able to talk above a whisper. He sat under the shade tree, giving energetic instructions with both hands, but he wasn't getting up much.

To service the old thresher, PJ went over the mechanicals with a grease gun. Junior swept the dust and chicken manure off the frame, checked the canvases and rolled out the big drive belt. Together, the two of them positioned the belt over the clutch of the John Deere and started it up, letting Pap see and hear it run right there in the tractor yard. It creaked and groaned at first, blowing dust everywhere, but once it got going it was a smooth-running machine.

It pained PJ to think of Pap never again working the farms on the Prairie, an event that used to create so much noise and dust that he and his schoolmates would climb up on the roof of the feed room at the back of the store just to see it at work in the distance.

For this fall, PJ thought it would more likely be Lee Junior who was pulling the rig down the road, working the peanut fields under Grandee's directions. And maybe he would himself be lucky enough to be there doing a man's work.

Granny Purdee came over from the big house to see what they were up to. "From all the noise that you all have been making, I figured you must be out here helping Pappy make a complete fool of himself," she said as she approached. "PJ, I would appreciate it if you and Junior will help me with a little job I need you to do up at the house?"

Because nobody ever turned down Claire Ruth Purdee, they both nodded in agreement, without even thinking to ask her husband if it was all right for them to abandon his project to take care of hers.

"Sure, Gran, what do you need us to do?"

"I need you two to climb up into the attic and get my door knobs back."

The two boys immediately looked at each other, as if to say: "Do we really want to do that?" They had done this job once before, and neither of them wanted to do it again. But who could say no to Grandee?

PJ's grandmother raised chickens in a henhouse out back. About a year before, when some of her eggs had come up missing, she had figured out that chicken snakes were the culprit. Grandee's solution had been to put white porcelain doorknobs in each nest. But now, even the doorknobs were disappearing.

That's when she asked the two boys to go help her locate them.

The Purdee's big house was a two-story wood structure with a large attic. The whole house, except for the concrete porch and its foundation, had been constructed of longleaf pine lumber that had likely been cut right out of the local forest, which was now called the cutover.

On certain nights, the grandmother had been hearing

crunching sounds coming from the attic. That was why she asked PJ and his friend Lee Junior to come climb up the ladder from the upper bedroom – the one PJ and Roy slept in on weekends when their mother was away.

At the top of the ladder was a trap door built into the ceiling of the closet that allowed them access to the attic. Once their eyes got adjusted to the subdued light up there, they could hardly believe what they saw. Just above their heads were dead chicken snakes hanging from the rafters, a sight scary enough to give each of them nightmares.

Summoning their courage to look further, PJ and Lee Junior discovered that the chicken snakes had been bringing the eggs they had swallowed up into Grandee's attic. They were cracking the eggs by crawling head first through holes in the knotty pine rafters supporting the roof.

But ceramic eggs will not break. Some of the snakes were five to six feet long, and the porcelain doorknobs were pushed to the very end of their tails. Without the strength to work their way back up through the knothole, they expired from hunger and exhaustion. So, PJ had climbed up on Lee Junior's shoulders and, with his pocket knife, cut each of their tails off, allowing their dried-out carcasses to fall to the attic floor on one side of the board, and the door knobs to fall to the other.

Neither of these young men wanted to go through that experience again. At least this time they had some idea of what they would find in Grandee's attic.

PJ and Lee Jr looked at each other in agreement. Lee Junior spoke for the two of them, "Yes, Ma'am, we'll come over in just a little bit."

When PJ's grandmother married Everett "Snappy" Purdee, mechanic at the gin shop and driver of the local school bus, she already was a successful manager of her family's farm. PJ wasn't clear exactly why his grandfather never took over those farm responsibilities, but it was obvious that his grandmother was in charge of the house and farm. Snappy just kept on with the school bus and his job as "Mr. Fix It" at the gin shop.

So far as PJ knew, Snappy never was a cotton farmer, and certainly never kept the Purdee family books.

They had a single son, Rayford, but Claire Ruth and her husband were cut from very different pieces of cloth. She was a manager; he wasn't a person who could be managed. She hadn't given up trying, but she had long ago realized that getting him to do what she wanted was a fruitless effort.

Sandy Prairie people knew that PJ's pap took an occasional vacation with the whiskey bottle. Last time it happened was in October, just after he collected his peanut checks. Having got himself liquored up across the River at the Channel Cat Saloon, he managed to get within a mile of home before driving his pickup into a fence.

Bert Pixley heard it and found Snappy P slumped over the steering wheel, his face down hard against the horn. Bert took him home to Claire Ruth and helped her get him into bed.

PJ's grandmother made no apologies. She had the attitude that the locals were as responsible for her husband's bad behavior as he was, and PJ thought perhaps they were. There was hardly a friend on the Prairie who would not have gone behind Gran's back, as PJ and Mr. Beeman found themselves doing, to sneak him some hard mash liquor or an occasional pack of cigarettes.

In his presence, Grandee never brought up the subject of liquor, nor did her husband. People used to joke about it, but never in front of Gran.

Pap cut an interesting figure. He always did his hair short, a bush cut that made his hair stand straight up. It gave him a fierce look. Perhaps because he was sensitive about his height – he was strong but not tall – Snappy P tore the sleeves out of his shirts to reveal his broad shoulders and Popeye arms. And he always wore a folded red bandana around his head.

PJ remembered Pap's arms and hands, thick and scarred, often sporting a cut or deep bruise, that as a little boy, he would inquire about. Pap's response would be, "Christ A'mighty boy, if you paid notice of every little nick you might as well stay in the house."

If PJ was helping him in the shop and brought him the

wrong tool, he would glare at him and say, "Christ A'mighty, boy, don't you know the difference between a Stillson and a Crescent wrench?" But then he would smile and give him a big hug. The boy knew his grandfather loved him. It was just his way of teaching him the things he needed to know, since his own dad was not there.

Snappy liked taking machines apart to see how they work and putting them back together again. He did that with his own tractor and peanut thresher, and with the bulldozer and silage harvester belonging to Cyrus Sapp.

He was a blacksmith and welder and liked to make tools. "Isn't she a sweetheart," Pap would say, patting the teeth of a 10-foot harrow he had just fabricated from scrap iron and painted a bright red. But what Pap admired from afar was airplanes. It was his great regret that he never got to work on one. He did get a close-up look at the Navy trainer that belly-landed in the Ketney's cotton patch on the Prairie during the war. But the Navy put a 24-hour guard on that plane before his Pap got very far into taking the engine apart.

PJ thought maybe that was why his grandfather was so proud when his son joined the war effort as a U.S. Air Force bombardier. PJ was still too little to remember much at all, but he had often been told what his pap said at the time, "You know you have done something when your kids can serve their country."

PJ's father never came home from the war, so neither Grandee or his mom ever had the same feeling that flying a plane for the Navy or the Army was something to be happy over. Pap's view was, "Sometimes you live your whole life and never get a chance to do anything like that. He got his chance."

As his Pap's death got nearer, PJ became more aware of his grandfather's aversion to churches. Grandee consulted with Belle about it: "Daughter, he won't talk about it because he doesn't want to have anything to do with any funeral if it is going to be religious."

"In my own mind, I am not convinced that we should be burying him in a church he never attended. He's already begging me, 'Don't you take me over there and have people say things they don't mean. I don't want to be made out to be something in death that I wasn't in real life.'"

Grandee said, "I would like to respect his wishes, but what can you do?"

"Christ, we are all going to die," Pap had told PJ out by the tractor shed. He was grinning through his pain and coughing for breath when he said it. "Some of us are already dead. They just haven't put us away yet."

"Seeds?" Mr. Beeman asked at the store, not believing. "He wants vegetable seeds, now?"

"Yes sir." PJ was at the counter. "Pap's set on planting a garden."

"A garden? He's never even had a garden. You can't plant a garden in the heat of the summer. It won't come up. It won't have time to produce anything."

"Yes sir, that's what Grandee told him. She said right out, `Pappy, that's foolishness.' But he don't listen. He's having Lee Junior plow him up a garden right beside the tractor shed. And he's going to plant it."

Mr. Beeman studied for a moment. "Seeds. . . mmm. I'll look and see what I've still got around here. What's he want?"

PJ pulled the list out of his pocket and gave it to the proprietor of the store. He had written each item down as his Pap had told him to: corn, tomatoes, okra, turnip greens, collards.

Mr. Beeman took the list from him and looked at it. "Is he going to live long enough to get these in the ground?"

PJ shook his head. "I don't think that's what matters."

Mr. Beeman knew the truth of it, and said, "Well, come with me to the feed room. Let's see which of these seeds I've still got back there."

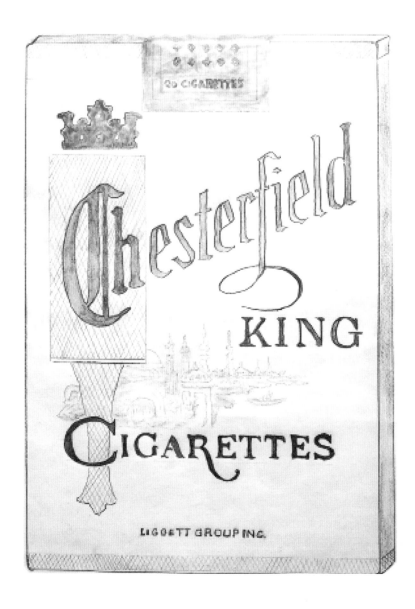

THE PICTURE SHOW

Whenever PJ and his brother Roy were hoeing, or picking cotton, or waiting for the school bus, or walking home from the store, they talked about movies they had seen at last Saturday's picture show.

All week long they talked over who the stars were and what they did, looking forward to the next Saturday show. The movies were about the only reason their family ever went into Theodosa.

PJ wanted to be able to share that with Lee Junior, too. Naming all the movie stars, repeating what they said. He wanted Junior and him to have more in common to talk about when they worked together.

Now that PJ was 14 and, as people frequently told him, "almost grown," he was confident that those opportunities would occur more often now.

He told Junior he wanted him to go with them to the picture show on Saturday night.

"How do you know yo momma want me to go?" Lee Junior had said when PJ suggested it. "Has you done asked her?"

"It won't hurt nothing," PJ told him.

"Well you best ask her."

On Wednesday, Lee Junior showed up on PJ's porch during supper. He explained that the clutch was messed up on his tractor, and he was asking Miss Belle if PJ might come turn the flywheel for him as he re-set the timing. The grease on Junior's shirt was about as black as he was. He wouldn't come in, but he did take a piece of pie.

Seizing the opportunity, PJ asked, "It'd be all right if Lee Junior comes with us to the picture show on Saturday, wouldn't it, Momma?"

"Goodness yes. That'd be fine, Junior."

"See there," PJ said.

Lee Junior had his tractor parked over at the gin shop. By the time the two of them got there, it was already dark and there wasn't any electric power going into the building. The transformer on the pole outside the shop must have gone out again. Neither of them could see a thing.

Lee Junior struck a match and looked around for the lantern. He found it, but there wasn't enough coal oil in it to light the wick. Junior decided the only way to solve the problem was for him to go home and get some more kerosene. He apologized to PJ for making him wait, and took off at a run.

Just outside the gin shop there was a butane tank. PJ climbed up and sat straddling it, his lungs sucking in the cool night air moving onto the Prairie.

His mind turned to thoughts about his Pap. In this old building, for so many years, his grandfather had worked on all kinds of mechanical devices, those that had been brought to him to work on and numerous other machines of his own invention.

PJ then thought some about Mr. Sapp and his cotton gin - that enormous mechanical structure set back from the big gin yard along side of the road. And how it was that the school, the church, the store and the gin shed all came to be positioned here at the Crossroads.

He thought about the farm families who brought in cotton for ginning. And how much they all counted on that single crop to pay for their family's expenses for a whole year.

He was also wondering whether or not those who ran the cotton gin would be asking him to once again to help run the suction, where forced air was used to pull the recently-picked cotton off the trucks and wagons as they took their turn on the weighing scales?

Since he now had a more personal relationship with Mr. Sapp, maybe the gin crew would give him more opportunities to help out at the press, the last important step in producing a clean white bale of lint cotton. He did some of that kind of work last year, as a helper to his new friend Guy Stookey. To be working the press again was what he most wanted to do.

He thought about Mr. Beeman and those who came into the store, people he knew at church, classmates at school. What he tried not to think about was leaving the Prairie. His mother was unhappy. He knew that for sure. What other kinds of work could she do? He had no good ideas about that.

He knew he was now big enough to help out. He was bringing in some money. He was thinking maybe - with his help - Belle could quit her job. Then she wouldn't have to ride that 30 miles over to the plant every day and come home at nights smelling of tallow and chicken entrails.

She could take some time off and they could go together as a family to those places she was always reading about and dreaming of, like South Carolina, Georgia and Florida.

What if he and Lee Junior were in business together? Pap had helped PJ start up a boiled peanut business. Peanut growers let him pick up some of their still-green peanuts, freshly turned up from the ground with the shells not yet dry and hard.

He took them home to clean and boil in salt water and dried them out in the oven. These he packaged in small paper bags he got from Mr. Bee at the store and carried around in his back pack. Nobody else is doing this, he thought. Five cents a bag is not a lot, but it adds up.

Lee Junior is growing garden vegetables as a cash crop. Junior's mother Nettie has her whole family picking purple hull peas and shelling and packaging them for sale. If PJ could borrow or rent Mr. Sapp's old truck, he could help the Johnson family enough to earn a share of the proceeds.

PJ had been thinking for some time about watermelon juice. He had already asked Mr. Sapp why he thought it was that there wasn't a watermelon drink that you could buy in the store, something like the strawberry cream soda that Mr. Bee liked so much.

He asked the same question of the grocer. "Watermelons are easy to grow, and they have a lot of sweet juice in them," he told Mr. Beeman. "And they are bound to be a lot better for you than

Cokes and Dr. Peppers that have all that sugar in them."

He decided he would talk some more with Joe Truehaw about this idea. "There's bound to be good money in fresh fruits and vegetables," he told himself.

PJ's thoughts returned to the idea of Lee Junior going with him and his family to the picture show. That would be something to look forward to. But he was worried about where Junior would sit. If they were to be partners in business they ought at least to sit together at the Saturday night movie.

He thought about the coming attractions, scenes from Red Rider and Little Beaver, one of the main features at the picture show. And he thought about the predicament Clyde Beatty of *Bring them Back Alive* had gotten himself into in the weekly serial. How would he escape from the tiger trap he had fallen into, which is where they left the animal trainer at the end of the last show?

Far down the road, he could see a light. It was bobbing like a cork on water. "That must be Junior," PJ thought to himself. "He's still running."

PJ held the light while Junior worked. It wasn't easy because his friend and mentor kept moving around from one side of the tractor to the other, from the tractor to the workbench.

He dropped a cotter key in the sand of the earthen floor. They had to get down on their hands and knees to find it.

"I don't see that many movies," Junior said in answer to PJ's question.

"Jimmy Wakely, you like him?"

"I guess so."

"Lash Larue?"

"Um. Don't know about him."

PJ was a good helper. He knew that. He made a study of figuring out what people needed before they needed it. He saw Lee Junior was looking around for something. He handed him the crescent wrench. He was right. It was exactly the tool his friend needed at that moment. PJ gathered up all the cotter keys and held them in his hand until Junior was ready for them.

"Which cartoons you like best?"

"Mr. McGoo, is he one?"

"Yeah, I like him. But the Road Runner's my favorite."

PJ did some Mr . Magoo and Bugs Bunny imitations. Lee Junior seemed to like those. It was satisfying to know Junior was actually coming on Saturday. It was really something to think about, to look forward to.

The movie theater in Theodosa had two public entrances, the main one at the front and one at the side. You stood in one line or the other to get your tickets, depending on whether you were white or colored. The side door led upstairs to the projection room and the balcony where the Negroes sat.

PJ waited until people started in. He was fourth or fifth in line on the colored side. When he stepped up and slid his money under the glass, the man in the ticket window looked up. "You on the wrong side, ain't you?" he said, studying PJ.

Under the fluorescent lights, PJ's hand looked even whiter than white was supposed to look. He had pulled the bill of his cap low over his eyes, it was the new John Deere cap that Mr. Sapp had given him.

PJ had made sure he wasn't the first one in line. He had his change ready, hoping the ticket man wouldn't notice.

There was uneasy movement in the dim hallway behind him. Lee Junior was next in line. Other colored were waiting to get their tickets. PJ realized he should have let Junior buy the ticket for him.

"It's all right," he heard his mother Belle say from the whites' side. Through the glass window of the ticket box he could see Belle and Roy standing in line.

"Albino," she said. "Everybody thinks he's white."

He couldn't believe she actually said that . . . What an awful thing to say.

The ticket man didn't pick up the money. "Ain't I seen you on the other side?" he said. He wasn't angry or anything. He just seemed curious to know if he was right. "You been here before, ain't you?"

Belle spoke up. "You must be thinking of somebody else," she told him from the other side.

"Yeah, you're thinking of somebody else," Roy said, moving up to the window on the "Whites Only" side.

The ticket man saw that the white boy pretending to be black was holding up the line. "Well, it's no difference to me," he said, "but you got to be one or the other." He tore off the ticket and slid it out to PJ. "You can't be goin' in both sides."

PJ moved onto the stairs and started up. He glanced back to see if Lee Junior was coming up behind him. For a moment, he had to put his arm against the wall as he was a bit unsteady and weak in the knees. He felt like he did when he had been caught in a driving rain and there wasn't enough air to breathe.

"Could we git some popcorn?" Lee Junior asked when the man gave him his ticket.

"How many you want?" the ticket man inquired.

"Two," Lee Junior told him.

"Zelma," the man called across the lobby, "two popcorns out here."

"It'll be jest a minute," he said.

Lee Junior stepped aside and signaled to PJ, the way they did when they were cutting silage or working at the cotton gin and nobody could hear because of the noise all that machinery made. His signal showed that everything was under control.

The ceiling lights were on inside the theater. People were still coming in. There were four rows of balcony seats, divided into three sections. The middle section was full, so Lee Junior and PJ went all the way across and took seats on the front row. The colored noticed him and whispered among themselves.

His belly voice kept signaling. "PJ," it said, "you're not supposed to be in this place. If you don't stop acting this way you're going to get us in bad trouble." PJ tried to think about other things.

The popcorn was salty and dry. He wanted a drink of water, but the thought of moving from where he was in his balcony seat was worse than being thirsty.

Peeking over the ledge, he looked to see where his mother and his brother were seated. There was Roy, standing up by his seat. He gave a big wave and said, "How's the air up there, brother?"

At least half the people in the floor below turned around in their seats. They were looking right up at him. PJ pulled quickly back, sat up straight and looked only to the front.

PJ had heard of people making things happen just by thinking about them. He concentrated on the blank screen. If he wished hard enough for the show to start, maybe it would.

"You wants to go down?" Lee Junior asked him quietly.

PJ shook his head.

"It'll be all right."

But PJ felt incapable of moving from where he was.

"They ought to have started this thing by now," PJ said as he glanced up behind him at the little room where the movie projector was. He could see the operator moving around inside.

"Looks like he getting things ready," Junior said. He had been to the picture show in Theodosa, but not often, and not recently.

"The cartoons come on first," PJ reminded him, speaking almost in a whisper. He tried to do an imitation of the opening of Looney Tunes for Junior, but it didn't come out right.

"What number serial is it? You was telling me it was Mr. Clyde Beatty in Darkest Africa, or something like that?"

"Number four, I think," he said, keeping his voice low. "Last week it left off with Clyde Beatty getting knocked down into his own trap. A tiger was going right for him. He has to git out of that."

"Maybe he won't git out?"

PJ had to look at him to see if he was serious. "Aw, he'll git out. That's the way they make these things."

"You come more'n just on Saturdays?"

"One time we came over here on a Sunday to see *King Solomon's Mines*." Mindful that others could hear, he said. "This place was completely full, at least down below. I don't know how many was up here. That's about the only time we come when it's not Saturday."

"But you likes the cowboy movies best."

"I like all kinds. But if I had to choose I'd choose Saturday night. You get more for your money. You get the cartoons, the newsreels, the serials, the coming attractions, and the main show all for one money. Sometimes they even have a double-feature."

"Looks like this evening is going to make lots for us to talk about.

"It is, you'll see."

Junior and PJ were already standing outside when Belle and Roy came out with the white crowd.

"Mom," PJ called out in a half-whisper from the shadows where they were waiting just off the sidewalk, "we're here."

Roy came ambling over. "Well, how was it?"

"It was all right," PJ said. He didn't know if Roy was referring to the show or to the fact that he was sitting up in the colored section.

"How about that darkie of Clyde Beatty's, Lee Junior? He's something funny, isn't he?" Roy stuck his rear out behind, rolled his eyes and looked scared the way Clyde Beatty's African helper had done.

Lee Junior's mouth came open like he was going to say something, but he didn't.

Roy asked, "Don't you wish you had a big gun like that elephant gun, Junior?"

The Negro in the serial was never of any help when Clyde Beatty needed him. His job was to carry the big gun, and he was supposed to have it ready. But whenever a wild animal got anywhere near, he threw the gun down and hid behind a tree. It had always seemed funny before, but this time PJ had noticed that all the laughs seemed to be coming from the floor below.

"I wouldn't know what to do with a gun like that, Roy," Lee Junior said.

"I would," Roy said.

Belle wanted to know. "What would you do with that kind of gun?"

PJ interrupted. "He would be out trying to blow the buzzards out of the sky. That's what."

"I bet I could with a gun like that," Roy agreed.

"Well, I hope you wouldn't," Belle said.

PJ told Lee Junior, "Roy's the only person I know, gets pleasure out of killing buzzards."

"I ain't killed that many."

"That's lucky for the buzzards," PJ said.

PJ saw his mother glancing over in the direction of the drugstore cafe. He didn't have to guess what she was thinking.

He had just thought about it, too. "We could just order some hamburgers to go," PJ said.

"Says who?" Roy demanded.

"We can't go to the cafe."

"Why the hell not?"

"Roy, you know very well why not. If we go to the cafe, Lee Junior won't be able to eat, that's why."

"Well, I'm not ready to go home."

PJ didn't see why Roy had to be so selfish. "There's more than just you to think about."

He realized he hadn't thought this part through. Somebody was going to have to come up with another idea. He turned to appeal to Lee Junior, but Junior was already walking away.

Belle was the first to call after him. "Junior, where you going?"

"I will just waits in the car," he told them.

"No, hold on, Junior. We'll all go to the cafe. We'll go together." Her voice was sincere, but it was almost as if she were trying to convince herself.

PJ certainly wasn't convinced.

"It's best y'all go ahead on," Junior said.

"No, it'll be all right," Belle told him. "We want you to come."

Roy said, "Come on, Junior. It'll be all right."

It was clear Lee Junior didn't want to. And PJ knew it wasn't all right. It wasn't all right at all. But Belle and Roy insisted. Once those two made up their minds there wasn't any changing them. There wasn't anything to do but go along and hope for the best.

Lee Junior walked with the three of them across the street, past the barbershop, the hardware store, and the Elks Hall. His freshly ironed white shirt glowed under each street lamp they passed.

If there was one thing true about Lee Junior, he was respectful. That's what people said about Lee Junior, "He's a good nigger," which in the Prairie community was quite a high standard, for it meant that he didn't talk back, he didn't go into places he wasn't wanted, and he knew how to give a full day's work.

Working hard, being respectful and knowing their place just went naturally together among Negroes to be admired.

PJ knew that Junior could have turned out different than he did. He had observed the colored spending their money on foolishness, never having anything of their own. But Junior wasn't like that. He dressed clean. He held his head up when you talked to him. He was polite. He had money left over when the bills were paid at the store.

The word was that Lee Junior gave Beryl Forkner cash for his old John Deere tractor. And he put down cash when he came in for seed and fertilizer at the store. And that would be in the spring of the year.

Mr. Beeman had said, "Nettie's family probably eats better'n yours and mine. When they come in here, they're not looking for the cheapest piece of meat in the case."

PJ speculated that Mr. Sapp's loan of money was what got Junior started with his own truck farm. But that was all right, because Lee Junior must have made enough selling tomatoes, turnip greens, collards and purple hull peas in town to pay it back several times over.

"He's clever," Joe Truehaw had said. "All these farms have gone over to cotton around here. Junior is smart enough to see that there's a need for somebody around here to grow something to eat."

That's why this going-to-the-café idea didn't make any sense. PJ suddenly came to realize that Junior would never be one to walk into some place in this town and order a Coca-Cola and a hamburger and get people upset by sitting down and eating it. It wasn't fair of his mother and Roy to put Junior into a situation like this.

Junior wouldn't be comfortable there. He wouldn't enjoy his hamburger. He would feel out-of-place. He would be out-of-place.

But fair or not, there they were striding up the steps of the cafe just like it didn't make a bit of difference in the world.

"Why, there's Belle," somebody said as she marched past the

people sitting up at the soda counter. "How you doin', Belle?"

"Fine. Jes fine," she said. "How y'all?"

She walked over and put her pocketbook on a table right in front of the window, the one where you could look out and see everybody drive by and they could look in and see you.

"It's about time you showed up, Belle." Franklin broke out from a covey of drugstore cowboys huddled around the jukebox. He picked up a glass on his way over and poured something in it from a sodawater bottle he had in his hand.

"Things'll liven up around here now," he said louder than he should have.

Belle gave him a hug. "My favorite drinkin' and dancin' partner," she said taking the glass and raising it in a toast.

"Here's to an eventful evening."

The cowboys and the domino players applauded. "I'm for that," Franklin agreed. "Here's to the most beautiful ex–basketball player in this cafe tonight." The crowd laughed.

"Drink up."

"My God, Frank, what did you put in this thing?" Belle coughed, trying to catch her breath. She stared at her coke as if she could see the liquor that was in it.

"It's a Coke special," her friend Franklin said, obviously enjoying the scene he had created. "We think it's an improvement on the recipe, don't we, Pate?

Pate steadied himself at every table and chair he came to on the way over. In his hand, he held a bottle of Delaware Punch. "You ain't tried anything until you tried mine," Pate said. He and Franklin both broke out in the giggles.

"I think I better pass on this," Belle said.

Franklin caught the poetry of it. "If it don't git you sooner, it'll git you later. Ain't that right, Pate?" The two of them laughed as if he had said something really funny.

"I better get these boys of mine something to eat." Belle turned and looked for them. They hadn't got much further than in the door. "Boys, what you doin' back there? Come on up here."

Ever since Roy walked in, he'd been acting like he'd come just by himself. All the time Belle was talking, Roy was giving extreme attention to the shelf of Milk of Magnesia bottles right by the entrance.

Lee Junior looked like he was trying to decide whether it was better to just walk out the door, or actually run. PJ felt certain it was better to run. Right now would be the time to do it. If Junior left, he wanted to be right behind him.

His mother called to them, "Junior, y'all come on and sit down."

The three of them filed past the people sitting on stools at the counter and went right to the table. PJ and Roy pulled out chairs and sat down. That left Lee Junior standing, his chest out, his shoulders back and his head turned slightly away like he might have been a waiter standing there waiting for them to place their order.

"Sit down, Junior," Belle told him. Junior was holding onto the chair and looking at it like it was stuck or something, but he didn't sit.

"Y'all know what you want?" Belle asked as if nothing whatsoever was wrong.

Roy grabbed the menu from between the catsup bottle and the sugar shaker. "I have to see what they got first."

It was the same menu Roy and PJ had gone over every Saturday. They could quote everything on it from the chicken fried steak to the pecan pie a la mode.

Besides, the two of them had already decided during the week what they were going to order. This was just Roy not wanting to face up to what he had gotten them into. PJ had both fingers and as many toes crossed under the table hoping that his mother knew what she was doing.

"Sit down, Junior," Belle said again.

Junior half-sat, the way you do when you have a risin' on your behind and dare not put your full weight down on it.

Sit down, Junior," Roy hissed from behind his menu.

Junior sprang up. "I'll jes waits in the car." It was a plea for mercy.

Patsy came over and wiped the oilcloth covering of the table with a wet rag. "Y'all ready to order now." She was trying hard not to see Lee Junior, even though he was right in front of her.

"I am," Belle said. "Fix me up a liver and onion sandwich. Have them slice that liver real thin and cook it done. I want some fried potatoes. You know how I like 'em, crisp."

"Any thang to drank?"

"I'll have a Nehi orange in a glass."

Frankie and Pate had stopped giggling. The domino players had stopped playing. The people at the counter had stopped eating. The whole place had stopped. Even the jukebox had run out.

"What you want, PJ?" Patsy asked.

"I'll jes have a Coke," he said. He didn't know why he said that. He didn't even like Coke. Coca-Cola was the last thing he ever would have ordered.

"What you doin'!" Roy demanded in that voice he used when he thought somebody was an idiot. "That's ridiculous. Order something to eat."

"Keep your voice down," Belle told him.

"What would you like?" Patsy asked Roy, skipping right past Junior.

"I'll have a cheeseburger. Without onions. I'll have fried potatoes, the skins left on. And I'll have a peppermint milkshake." That was what he said earlier in the week he was going to have and that's what he ordered. Looking at the menu didn't change that.

"Will that be all?"

"No, Patsy, that's not all," Belle said.

"What else you want?"

"You haven't asked Lee Junior what he wants."

Patsy didn't look at Lee Junior at all. She looked right at the woman she used to go to high school with. "Is it to go?"

"No, he's going to eat it right here with us."

She shook her head. Belle and Patsy were eyeball to eyeball. "I can't serve him."

"You can't?" Belle said it the way she might have said to a lady she went to school with that ran a beauty parlor, like "What do you mean you can't do my hair?"

"No."

"Well, I tell you what." Belle was getting heated up. PJ could see that. "I'm all of a sudden feeling real hungry. Go ahead and bring me my liver and onions but, on the side, bring me a hamburger with everything on it, onions and all and make me a big malted milk. That's in addition to the Nehi orange."

The waitress said, "All right," and left.

Belle turned in her seat. "Now let's see why it's so quiet in here. Frankie, how come you let the music run out?" Franklin just stood there looking at her like he didn't know this woman at all.

Belle took a quarter out from her pocketbook and tossed it right at him. He reached and caught it, but he didn't do anything with it.

Wesley Tharp, the proprietor, came out of the kitchen heading straight for their table. He was trying hard to keep his voice under control. "Belle, you tryin' to ruin me?"

"No, Wesley."

"You are. You're goin' to do it."

Belle was trying to be calm too. "Junior, just go ahead and sit down."

Junior sat down. His eyes were large, showing white, his pupils rolled around just like the African in the Clyde Beatty serial. Only it wasn't funny. The tigers were real. It wasn't Saturday at the movies. It was Saturday night at the café, and the danger was so heavy you could smell it.

"Service is usually pretty good aroun' here, Wesley. It's a little slower tonight for some reason."

"Belle, what am I supposed to do?"

"You might put some music on. It's so quiet in here it's pathetic." She looked around. "Franklin doesn't look like he's in too good a mood either."

Franklin came up and placed the quarter on the table. "What you tryin' to prove, Belle?" Pate was right behind him, and behind the two of them, the domino players and others formed a circle.

"Excuse me," Belle said, "I thought this was a cafe."

Pate said to Lee Junior, "Boy, you better git up out of that chair."

Junior jumped immediately up. His chin was tucked in and his neck muscles bulged like he was prepared to take blows on the top of his head. PJ got up as well.

"I guess you folks haven't met my oldest boy," Belle declared.

"He's not any boy of yours," Franklin said, "And you know it."

"If I say he is, he is."

"This is getting ridiculous," Franklin said to Wesley Tharp as if he had figured out it was some kind of joke. He laughed, "Belle, your idea of fun is pretty weird."

Belle stood up. "If Junior doesn't sit, don't none of us sit. Git up, Roy."

Roy got up.

"Why you doin' this, Belle?" one of the domino players wanted to know. He must have been thinking there was something he had missed.

"This ain't no Christian community, Wesley," Belle said, shaking her head.

PJ had no idea why his mother said that.

"He don't want to be here," Pate said. "Look at him."

Junior was holding onto the back of his chair as if he were facing a wind that could pick him up and turn him end over end and send him off flying through the air.

Franklin said with an edge to his voice, "You better head up North, Belle. Moving to somewhere else in the South is not goin' to be to your liking neither."

Wesley took charge. "I tell you what. You just stand right here. I'm going to go make up those burgers just like you ordered them. Then you can take them with you. This order will be on me."

Wesley had already turned to go when Belle said, "Don't inconvenience yourself Wesley. We are leavin'."

Belle burned rubber getting the car out of the picture show parking lot. Her hand lay hard on the horn as she drove them past the barbershop and the hardware store and the Elks Hall. She honked all the way out of town.

"Damn," she said, "I made a holy mess out of that." "Damn. Damn."

PJ could tell she was too mad to cry.

The Cutover

A late summer thunderstorm up on the Prairie blew a gate open on the Sanstrom farm. The Widow Sanstrom's hogs got out and headed for the Cutover.

Next morning, Mrs. Sanstrom went to the store to seek advice from Mr. Beeman. Mr. Beeman talked to PJ, and PJ appealed to Joey Lou Truehaw for help. Joey Lou was the 17-year-old daughter of Joe Truehaw.

Joey Lou had farm work to do. She really didn't have time to deal with rounding up a bunch of hogs, but eventually brought Buzz, her milk cow dog, over in her pickup.

She and PJ drove as far as Evens Creek, then got out and tracked down the Sanstrom hogs on foot. They found seven of them down in the creek bed, and, with Buzz's help, they finally got them out onto the road heading toward the Prairie.

Joey Lou had to get back to work. She left in her pickup.

PJ and the dog spent most of the afternoon getting the hogs back into the Sanstrom pen. In appreciation, Widow Sanstrom sent PJ home with a jar of fresh buttermilk, that was for him, and a pound of butter, that was for Joey Lou.

"Tell that Truehaw girl I said, thank you. I so appreciate what you kids done." Had her shoats got further into the Cutover, she said, they could have been gone forever. And that would have been a real loss.

For local hog owners, the Cutover was commonly known as hog heaven." For some, it was another way of saying "gone forever."

A week later, a rider patrolling the Game Preserve pasture came across a sow that had what looked like the Sanstrom earmark: a crop and an over-bit cut in the left ear. The rider mentioned it to Mr. Beeman at the store, who conveyed the information to PJ, who ran over and told the news to Mrs. Sanstrom.

Widow Sanstrom confirmed that "yes, it's my sow that is still missing" and would sincerely appreciate his help getting the hog back.

PJ ran once again to find Joey Lou. She was busy bailing hay for Pootie Wilson and didn't want to hear anything more about the Sanstrom hogs.

Eventually, she agreed that PJ could come over to the Truehaw place and get the dog Buzz to help him.

When his mother got home from work, PJ told her what he was going to do the next day. "Honey, that sounds all right to me. You just be careful." He thought she sounded tired, but relieved that he had something constructive to do. He knew she felt bad leaving her boys home alone when they weren't in school.

In the early morning, PJ waited with his mother at the Crossroads store until the carpool arrived that would take her to work at the poultry processing plant in Theodosa. Once she was out of sight, he turned and ran full speed over to the Truehaw farm to retrieve the dog Buzz.

By the time the boy and the dog got to the bridge where the River road crossed Evens Creek, the sun was already high. Buzz scented some tracks, but those were not fresh. Together they worked their way east, mostly walking in the creek bed, since it had very little water in it and was a natural opening into the thicket.

With high humidity and no breeze at all, dog and boy each were feeling the heat. The dog went ahead. In the underbrush, PJ was having a hard time keeping up. He heard a bark. Was the dog onto something? The bark was louder.

Maybe we have found our sow, PJ was thinking. PJ was moving more quickly, jumping over snags, and wading right through the creek mud.

From somewhere downstream he thought he heard a hog-like nasal sound, and then a screech and a squeal that had to be a hog. The dog was baying Hoo! Hoo! Hoo!, as if he had cornered something.

PJ pitched forward though the brush to get closer to try to see. He saw the back end of the dog, its legs spread wide, its nose pointed in the direction of a dark entanglement of shrubs and vines in the bed of the creek.

The dog looked back to see if PJ was there, and began using a different barking rhythm, a breathy Yip! Yip! Yip!

PJ moved forward but still couldn't see what it was. The dog moved forward too, but its voice changed to a low Grrrr! Grrrr! Grrrr! It looked like Buzz was going in. Then the vines and branches began to open from the inside, and something was coming out. It was something big, and it was not the Widow Sanstrom's sow.

In the creek bed with PJ was a razorback - a real piney woods rooter - a fierce-looking dinosaur of a hog covered with mud, with black wire-like hair standing straight up. This one's nose looked like the blunted head of a spike hammer of the type the railroad crews use in laying rails, and it had large ivory tusks curling out each side of its mouth.

The boy blinked his eyes, and the hair on his own neck began to stand up, the way such a fright had affected Clyde Beatty's Negro in the picture show. He held his breath. This was definitely not an animal you would see at the county fair, and this was not a movie serial where you were a safe distance away from the screen.

The hog was on the attack, moving toward the dog. PJ didn't know whether to try to protect the dog or to save himself. He opened his mouth to cry: "Buzz, don't!" when a man's voice above him commanded: "Dog back!"

On the embankment above, PJ was surprised and greatly relieved to see old Walter Wentforth on his horse Sport. But Buzz either didn't hear the command, or didn't recognize its meaning, for the big boar turned and went directly for the dog.

With a quick upward swipe of his head, the hog flipped Buzz into the air and the dog, yelping in pain, fell to the ground right at PJ's feet. The hog looked up, and PJ knew immediately that he was in trouble, and began to scramble up the creek bed.

Somewhere in his panicked flight, PJ heard the horseman's

voice give another loud and clear command, "Ret, catch!" And instantly there was another dog between PJ and the hog. The dog Ret leaped and attached himself to the boar's ear, pulling its huge head toward the ground.

"Fox, catch!" he heard the rider's voice say, and, as quickly, the dog Fox was clamped onto the other ear, helping to pull the animal's head into the muddy floor of the creek bed.

"Sorry, son. That's my hog."

Walter Wentforth dismounted his horse and came down into the creek. He held a lariat rope in one hand and a rifle in the other. In one quick gesture, he pointed the rifle barrel at the head of the hog and pulled the trigger.

The sound of the gunshot and the death squeal of the hog rose up from the cavity of the creek and dissipated slowly into the mantle of the forest.

"Ret, Fox. It's okay. Lay down, boys," he said to his dogs. They lay down on either side of the dead hog, panting.

Walter placed the point of a Bowie knife just under the flapping jowls of the hog and push hard downward, letting red blood gush out onto the sand and gravel of the creek.

He looked up to where PJ was holding onto a broken branch of a willow tree. To PJ, he said, almost apologetically, "I been tracking this fellow. You just got to him afore I did. Sorry about your dog, son."

PJ, trembling all over, climbed back down into the creek bed and knelt beside Buzz. To Mr. Wentforth, he said, "This isn't even my dog. Its Joey Lou Truehaw's."

His voice came out kind of shaky. "We were looking for the Widow Sanstrom's sow." Tears smarted in his eyes.

Walter came over to where PJ was and put a hand on his shoulder. "Let's see what we can do for the dog."

The old man turned and climbed up the embankment to where his horse was waiting.

PJ watched him as he put the rifle back into its scabbard at the saddle, and come quickly back to where he was. Mr. Wentforth brought with him a small corked bottle, a large needle and some heavy thread.

PJ held the head of the borrowed dog in his lap. He was bleeding along the shank of his left hind leg and from his chest where his ribs were showing through.

Mr. Wentforth wiped at the wounds with a rag from his pocket. He then poured something PJ thought might be spirits of alcohol along the cuts where the hog's tusk had ripped Buzz open.

When he set these aside, he proceeded to pull the skin together and sew the dog up right there.

The dog was whimpering and kicking and tossing his head. It was all PJ could do to hold him down. Nobody spoke during the operation. They were all suffering from the breezeless heat of the midday sun.

An awful smell came off the hog and enveloped the close space around them. PJ thought that falling into the hole of an outhouse must be something like this.

Mr. Wentforth then turned his attention to the razorback. He picked up the lariat rope and wrapped one end of it around the nose of the dead hog, locking onto its tusks to secure it.

Climbing out of the creek, he tied the other end of the rope to the horn of the saddle on his horse. With a single command, "Sport. Pull!" the horse dragged the maybe 300-pound hog – by its two-and-one-half-inch tusks – right up out of the creek.

The horseman then untied the rope from the saddle horn, retied it to the horse's tail and backed away. "Sport. Go home!" On this command, the horse left without a rider, dragging the hog by its tail.

Ret and Fox were resting side by side in the shade of the creek bed, and PJ was cradling Buzz in his lap when Mr. Wentforth returned. He sat down in the blood-soaked sand beside them. "She'll be back after a'while," he said, referring to the horse. "Then we can all go home."

As they sat talking in the sandy bed of the creek, PJ learned several things that he thought might be important to know.

According to Wentforth, "a good hog dog is worth ten cowboys in the woods. This breed of dog – the cur dog – is good at picking up a scent," he told PJ. "They are excellent trackers, and they know to wait until you get there. They know their own names and act only on your command."

"Their make-up is to please you," he continued. "The cur dogs are real smart and pretty near fearless, so it's you who has to decide to send 'em in, or not. They will look at you to see what you are looking at. They will listen for your voice to know what you want them to do."

But he also warned, "You've got to use this kind of dog every day, or they will go off on their own. You can't have that."

Walter Wentforth explained to PJ that he always inspects his dogs to see if they are hurt. If they are, "I may wash their wounds with warm water. I sometimes use alcohol to disinfect it, or I just let the dog lick it. Sometimes one dog will lick another's cut. That cleans 'em up about as good as anything."

About three quarters of an hour later, the horse Sport reappeared and stood looking down into the creek as if to see whether the man, the boy and the dogs were still there.

Scrambling up the creek bank was hard for PJ, trying not to let loose of Buzz, who was heavy to carry and not cooperating.

The first thing PJ did when he got to where the horse stood waiting was to look to see whether or not the horse still had its tail.

The lariat rope was nowhere to be seen, but a pair of saddlebags had been hung onto the saddle. Mr. Wentforth opened one and took out an animal bladder that had been filled with water. He gave PJ a drink then drank some himself. He poured some of it on a ragged bandana that he was using to clean his knife. He dribbled some the water on his hands and let his dogs lick them dry.

As it turned out, Walter Wentworth's sister Molly, whom PJ already knew, had been waiting with the family pickup truck and trailer all this time over on the River road.

"Molly!" Walter called. "We got a hurt dog. Give us a little help out here will you?"

Molly climbed out of the truck as they came up. "PJ," she said, calling him by name, "Is your dog hurt bad?"

"Its not my dog, Miss Molly." PJ quickly explained, "This is Joey Lou Truehaw's cow dog Buzz. We were looking for a lost sow."

Molly came quickly over to take a look. She said, ""PJ, I think we better take this dog home with us. We'll need to keep a watch over this one."

That's what Molly advised PJ to do, and PJ wasn't in a position to argue with her.

After Walter loaded Sport into the horse trailer, PJ climbed into the bed of the truck and sat down next to the stuck hog. The stench was so awful he covered his nose with his shirt tail across his arm. Walter lifted Buzz onto PJ's lap.

Then, the Wentfort pickup truck with the horse trailer following behind headed for their home place.

Walter and his widowed sister Molly lived on a sandy hill setback into a brushy thicket on the edge of the Cutover. There were two unpainted houses set side by side, one for Walter and one for Molly.

The siblings shared a common barn, a slaughter shed, a smokehouse and a large hog pen bound in by heavy wire mesh supported by old railroad crossties as posts. The Wentforths made their living from hogs they caught wild from the woods, and from what they raised. They seasonally released their hogs to fatten on acorn mast found in the surrounding thicket, and recaptured them in the late fall and winter.

The Wentforths always had pork for sale, in the form of lard, salted ham, sugar-cured bacon, stuffed and smoked sausages and chitlins. Their customers drove down from the Prairie to purchase their supplies of meat, or they bought them from the Crossroads store that stocked those same Wentforth products.

Walter Wentforth pulled the truck right up into the yard. Molly hurried onto the front porch and shook out a deer hide rug for the dog Buzz to be laid down on. "Y'all go ahead and bring that hurt dog up onto the porch," she said.

Walter helped PJ lift Buzz out of the truck and together they carried him up the steps. They laid him gently down on the rug.

"You boys must be famished," Molly said. "Go get yourselves cleaned up out there at the well house, I'll have some venison stew warmed up for you pretty soon. PJ, will you stay?"

Yes, Ma'am. Thank you so much."

Molly grabbed a couple of washrags from the clothesline strung across the porch and tossed them in their direction.

The dogs, Ret and Fox, were still standing at alert in the back of the pickup truck, waiting for Walter Wentforth's command. Eventually he noticed them and said: "Hit's ok boys. On the porch." And they jumped off the truck, came up on the porch and lay down.

Walter sat down in a straight chair to untie the laces of his riding boots. He pulled them off, along with his socks, and propped his bare feet up on the banister for a good "airing out."

PJ, feeling responsible, sat down beside Buzz on the porch floor.

Molly brought out a tray with three bowls of stew and some fresh-made crackling bread. These she set on the bench.

"Thank you, Molly," Walter said. "Hit sure smells good."

Miss Molly went back inside the house and promptly returned with a pitcher of sweet tea and some glasses for the three of them. She then chose a handmade hickory rocking chair as the place to have her meal.

Walter, the talker of the family, drank about half the tea in his glass before he was reminded of a story he wanted tell. "PJ, have you ever seen a drunk hog?"

"No, sir, I don't think I have," PJ grinned, stroking Buzz with the back of his hand. He had shared more than one meal on this porch and knew that it was a place for the telling of tales. "But if you want to tell me about it, I'll sure listen."

"I seen this one first hand," Walter said. "Winter before last, Phil Pharris started feeding his cows sweet sorghum silage. You may know about that, since he did it on the advice of your neighbor, Joe Truehaw."

"Mr. Truehaw convinced Mr. Pharris to set aside 40 acres

of his cotton ground, 20 acres for fenced pasture and the other 20 for the planting of a new variety of sorghum grass. His idea was that sorghum would produce a nice big head of grain and its stalks had a high-sugar content. Ground up, sorghum silage would make good cattle feed."

Walter told PJ, "All that seemed to work out for Pharris. The cows fared well on the summer and fall pasture. And the sorghum grew tall in stalk and did better than expected as a grain crop. Mr. Pharris needed to convert the sorghum into silage and store it for winter feeding, so he made a deal with the County Road Commissioner to dig him a trench silo that sloped away from his barn out back of the house."

"He also invested in a new John Deere chopper that he used to grind the sorghum into silage. He dumped all that silage into the ditch, and had his County bulldozer man push a layer of earth on top. He packed it down and sealed it, so air couldn't get to it."

"Winter came on, and rainwater soaked into the ground and made its way down into the silo. Pharris opened the lower end of the trench to let his cows try this new feed. Inside the silo, that wet fodder and those sorghum tops had fermented, giving off an odor so strong his wife wouldn't let him in the house until he changed his work clothes."

"But he knew it was worth it, because when he dug that sweet silage out and put it into troughs for his cows, they loved it and gained weight from eating it."

Walter drained the rest of his iced tea and continued his story. "That whole enterprise was such a success that even Bee Beeman at the store called it a miracle product. And he was soon encouraging Phil to add sulphur, salt and cottonseed meal from the store to make it the perfect winter feed for his cattle. And that's what Phil did."

"But then, Mr. Pharris noticed that something peculiar was happening with his chickens. His hens and one rooster had been pecking at the grains in the bottom of the trench and drinking the flavored water that seeped out of the silo. Those chickens would flap their wings and jump straight up in the air, like they meant to fly, but crashed back to the ground and couldn't always get up."

"What happened was that Pharris' chickens were intoxicated. Yes, they were absolutely drunk."

He had to pick them up one by one and shut them up in the pen to keep them from going off down there to his new silo."

In telling his story, Walter was using his hands and arms to show how the chickens were trying to fly, which made PJ laugh a lot.

It pleased him even more when Walter said, "Now, this story doesn't end with the chickens. I got called over there when some of our Cutover hogs found that silage."

"Here is what happened. It was February when Mr. Pharris opened his trench silo wider to dig out more of the silage to feed his cattle. One morning, when he was going down there, he caught a glimpse of a hog heading out across the sorghum stubble. He thought it was odd that the hog kept falling over, and getting up and falling over again.

Then he found a second hog on its knees no more than 20 feet from the opening in the silo. It was unable to get up.

"This one was a genuine black piney woods rooter, large and ugly. Its belly was bloated and dragging the ground as if its legs were too weak to hold up its body. The head was making a great effort to get its mouth open, which was the only thing about it that moved. Sweet sorghum juice and grain oozed out into a puddle where its head was resting in the grass."

That was when Mr. Pharris called on me and my horse to come over and take that hog away."

Mollie and PJ both enjoyed a laugh about that story. Even Buzz lifted his ears to hear what was going on, but he didn't get up. PJ asked if he could tell a story next, a story he had never told before.

Walter and Molly were both pleased that he felt comfortable enough to share with them a story of his own.

"Last November," he told them, "I was looking for a yearling belonging to one of your neighbors up on the River Road. You know Miss Eleanor. Well, her calf went missing.

Someone thought they had seen it in the hardwoods opposite her place. She gave that information to the mailman, who passed it on to Mr. Bee up at the store.

It was Mr. Beeman who asked me if I wanted to go over and help her out. Well, I went over there early on a Saturday morning. She showed me where the calf might have got out, and gave me a description of what it looked like."

PJ explained to the Wentforths, "It was real cold, but it was a clear day and the sun was shining. I remember there was a heavy frost cover on the weeds and grass along the edge of the woods. I was running, covering ground at a fast pace, dodging post oaks and briars and leaping over downed logs and small stream beds, as I like to do."

"But I stopped because I saw something glowing in the weeds there. It was a ball of ice."

With his hands, PJ showed that what he saw was a little bigger than a softball but not quite so big as a cantaloupe.

"I reached down and picked it up to look at it up close. It was very light in weight, but freezing cold. Inside were hollow chambers made of ribbons of ice folded into a ball."

"Since I didn't know what it was and had never seen anything like it, I decided to take it with me, and carried it for just a little while."

"I discovered pretty quick why that wasn't going to work. The ice was turning to water right in my hands, and my hands were freezing. I didn't really want to do it, but I just set it down on a nest of leaves and ran on."

"And I have never seen anything like that again."

PJ asked the two of them, "Have you ever seen anything like that?"

It was clear that the story meant something to Molly. She raised her hand and there was some excitement in her voice. "I know what that is. It's frost weed, PJ. That's what that is. My former husband and I saw it bloom only twice in our whole lives, years ago. I'm so happy to hear that it still happens."

Walter confirmed for his part, "I know I've never seen it, Sister."

Molly then explained what she knew. "The 'frost flower' blooms when freezing sap is pushed out of the stem of a weed that grows on the edges of the woods. It only happens," she said, "when there is a heavy frost in late fall and the sap turns into a ribbon of ice that curls in on itself."

"You have to be there when it happens," she explained, because when the sun hits it, it melts. Melted frost weed ice is just plain water."

It pleased PJ to learn from their explanation, and he accepted it as truth. But, inside, he was disappointed. He was wanting to think about his coming upon a chambered ball of ice in the woods as something mystical, perhaps an omen or message for him alone.

Maybe it still was. It could have been one of God's signs that PJ just did not know how to interpret.

Walter got up from his chair and poured some water from Molly's bucket into his empty soup bowl. He set it in front of the dog Buzz and tipped it a little so that it could drink.

When he dog began lapping up the water, Walter said, "That's a good sign."

Miss Molly began to rock and sing quietly to herself, as she often did. After a few phrases, Walter said, "Molly, would you turn that up a little bit, so we can hear it?"

Without a single moment of hesitation, Molly sang right out just like she was on the radio.

PJ had heard her sing before and loved it, especially when she sang the old favorites like "Good Night Irene," "Pretty Polly," and "The Old Rugged Cross."

Ret and Fox lay on their bellies, stretched out on the porch with their heads resting between their front legs. Sometimes the dogs sang along too.

PJ loved spending time on the Wentforth's porch. When they sang out loud, the whole woods around them were like a sponge sucking it in.

And as the good feeling of singing out-loud encompassed them, Miss Molly, her brother Walter, PJ and the two dogs all broke out in a full body sing-along:

O beautiful for spacious skies,
For amber waves of grain,
For purple mountain majesties
Above the fruited plain!
America! America! God shed His grace on thee,
And crown thy good with brotherhood
From sea to shining sea!

At the end of the song, the dog Buzz shook his head and struggled to his feet. PJ felt a wave of relief. "Good boy, Buzz!"

Late in the afternoon, Walter Wentworth dropped PJ and Buzz at the Truehaw place where the boy had some explaining to do. PJ was not certain how he might keep the day's events from being reported with any degree of detail to his mother, or even worse, to imagine what Mr. Beeman at the store would do with such a story.

THE COTTON GIN

PJ was working up at the press on the Saturday afternoon in October when Mr. Tom died.

He didn't see it happen. Beryl Forkner had been standing closest to him, but he didn't see it either. The first PJ knew anything was wrong was when somebody pulled the clutch on the drive belt and the vast machinery of the cotton gin came to a creaking halt right in the middle of making a bale of cotton.

PJ crouched at the top of the stairs trying to see what was going on. They wouldn't shut the gin down unless something was wrong. The first thought he had was: "fire in the cotton."

Fire was what they worried most about in a cotton gin. But he wasn't smelling anything like cotton burning, and there was no clanging of the bell.

He saw Beryl come hurrying back in from the engine room. The big diesel engine was left idling. He didn't know whether to go down or not.

PJ knew he could make good use of a few moments of down time preparing the next batch of metal ties. Also, the compress box wasn't set up yet. If they gave him a little more time, he knew he should run and get some more burlap bagging out of the seed house. He wanted to be ready when they started the gin up again.

He went over to the window by the cooling tower, hoping to better see from there what was happening. He could make out that Beryl was at the stands, where the big rollers and saws stripped the seed from the cotton. Beryl was bending over something on the floor, but PJ couldn't tell what it was.

Up there on the finishing platform was where PJ had most wanted to be, where the owners of the cotton came to see their year's work wrapped in burlap and bound by metal straps.

It would take at least 1200 pounds of seed cotton picked

in the field to make a perfect size bale of lint cotton at the gin. Hoisting the just-ginned bale up onto the scales for weighing and writing its weight into the record book were both part of PJ's new responsibilities. He especially wanted that job because up at the press was where the growers could see for themselves what their investment had produced.

A 500-pound bale of lint cotton was what they all hoped for, since that was what the big cotton buyers were expecting. And then there would be an additional amount for the cottonseed weighed out in the seed hopper, depending on whether or not the farmer wanted to keep his seed for planting in another year.

Sometimes whole families came up and stood before the press, watching the clean lint fold down into the massive wooden boxes. They stood to the side pointing in awe at the great trompers rising and falling, pressing down on the sponge-like cotton, their voices lost in the noisy din of whirring belts and pulleys, fans, blowers and saws.

This summer was the first time PJ was more than just a part-time helper at the press. He had paid close attention when Guy Stookey was operating the presses and now he was able to manage them by himself.

He liked everything about this job. He knew that he didn't understand exactly how the gin worked. He also knew he didn't have to, just as he didn't have to understand how his kidneys worked or how it was that the earth went around the sun while the moon went around the earth. Man and earth, sun and moon were part of a larger enterprise, larger than any one part. Just as his kidneys and his liver were a part of him, he was part of the press and the press was a part of the gin and the gin was a part of the community and not any of them could do without the other.

For PJ, cotton ginning was a whole new kind of work, so different from the manual labor of chopping cotton, or picking cotton, or hauling cotton in from the field.

It wasn't just the money or the responsibility or the attention. It wasn't like somebody just ran the suction, somebody ran the stands, somebody ran the press, somebody else ran the office. What was so extraordinary about the ginning of the cotton was the cleverness of it that made everything work together for a purpose. For him, the pleasure was being part of a local effort to do something important right there on the Prairie.

When each press was filled with lint cotton, PJ was now able to reach up to the lever and stop the big trompers poised just above the compress boxes. He was big enough now to muscle around the big wooden carousel all by himself, and throw open the doors, each as large as he was tall.

The key was that every piece of equipment was perfectly balanced, perfectly weighted, so that a single person could operate it.

It pleased him to see the onlookers shake their heads with wonder. Here was this young man and this big machine, so perfectly responsive, so perfectly suited to each other, helping to produce the cotton that shirts and pants were made of and the cottonseed that would be pressed into oil, or crushed into cow feed, or just taken back to the farm and planted in another year.

Mustn't it be true that he was now a man in his own right, if he was doing the work of two, if he had tied and weighed out every bale ginned since Guy Stookey left to go bring his wife back from wherever she was? Mustn't it be true if Mr. Sapp had told him to do the best he could and no one, not at the stands or the suction or anywhere in the whole operation, had had to let up for one second because of him?

And wasn't it obvious, even light-framed as they said he was, that he had worked out the timing just right so he could put the full force of both feet into rolling the finished bale of cotton down the platform, a back-straining quick shove to get it going, a half-flip from the press to the floor and a quick up-roll to the scales? A five-hundred-pound bale, more or less, rolled out every 30-minutes - that should be proof enough.

PJ could see from where he was that the usual white blanket of cotton was no longer flowing across the separating saws at the stands, down there where Beryl Forkner was looking around like he was expecting somebody to show up and do something.

PJ saw Lee Junior was now climbing down off the wagon

out front where he had been feeding the suction. He must have decided he had better go down. Mr. Sapp wouldn't like for the gin to be idling when there were cotton wagons waiting in line outside.

PJ arrived on the gin floor about a half-minute after Lee Junior and knew right away that something was terribly wrong. Junior' face was the color of ashes. He looked where Junior was looking. There was a person lying on the floor. He immediately recognized that it was Mr. Tom.

To PJ, it seemed like the old black man had just chosen an inconvenient place to take a rest. His eyes, wide open, seemed to be concentrating on something up in the rafters. Nothing about him moved.

"When I turned 'round, there he lay," Beryl said, thinking maybe he had to say something. He spoke loudly as if the gin were still running. The way he said it, it sounded like he thought somebody might blame him. He shifted his chew of Days Work tobacco from his lower to upper jaw. "I thank he's dead," he said as if to explain why Mr. Tom hadn't gotten up.

PJ wondered how you could tell.

"I seen him standin' there. People always do that. Stand right here in the way. Thinkin' you're not goin' to do it right when they don't know nothin' tall about it."

Beryl started to spit out some of his tobacco juice but found Mr. Tom lying where he was in the habit of expectorating, so he spit into the fire barrel. A mother of fine cotton lint and gin dust had settled on the water in the barrel. Beryl watched the brown liquid momentarily to see whether it would settle. "Next thang I knew he wus fell slap over."

PJ nodded sympathetically. He understood that Beryl did not want to be blamed. He knew too that, unlike himself, it bothered Beryl for people to watch him work and especially did not like for people to ask him a question.

Lucky for him, PJ thought, you just waste your breath trying to make yourself heard above all this gin noise.

Beryl seemed fidgety, as if the quietness was a threat that needed to be gotten done with. Lee Junior had backed away and was holding onto the wall. His muscles were trembling the way they were the night of the cafe.

Scared to death of dead people, the colored are, PJ reminded himself. Before now, he hadn't actually seen that for himself.

Mr. Tom didn't look much different than he always did. He was thin and the skin lay tight against the bones in his face. His pants legs had pulled up and PJ could see his spindly ankles above his worn-over Sunday shoes. He wasn't wearing socks.

PJ thought to himself that, as a general rule, skinny people aren't comfortable lying on hard floors, especially on a concrete floor like this. Their bones come through and their skin doesn't give them much cushion. But he had to admit, Mr. Tom did look quite relaxed and content with his head cradled up against the fire barrel and his legs extended out into the pass-by.

"Did you see it?" PJ asked Lee Junior. He thought it likely that, had his friend Junior been looking, he might could have seen what had happened. He had a good view of the stands from where he was feeding the suction up in the wagon. But Lee Junior shook his head. He was having a hard time getting his breath.

Curious, PJ asked Beryl, "You think he hit his head?"

"Could be," Beryl replied. "I wadn't payin' any attention to him."

Mr. Sapp came around from the office. Bert Pixley was with him. They were in a hurry. PJ knew automatically they would be wanting to know why somebody shut down the gin.

The gin never stopped until the last load of picked cotton was finished for the day, even if it was way into the night. Everybody knew that.

Cyrus Sapp, the owner and gin manager, had taken off his gold wire reading glasses and was trying to stuff them into the front pocket of his starched khaki shirt as he walked. That pocket was already full of pencils. When he arrived at the obstacle that lay in the middle of the walkway before the stands, he bent over and gave Mr. Tom a puzzled look.

From behind him, Bert asked of Beryl, "That's Arlyn Jones' nigger, ain't it?" At the same time, Mr. Sapp was wanting to know, "Is he dead?

"I don't know anything about it," Beryl said defensively.

Mr. Sapp looked over at Lee Junior. "This Mr. Tom's bale of cotton we're ginning, Lee Junior?"

"Yas suh. This one's his'n," he said, coming in a little closer to where the body was.

Lee Junior didn't have a shirt on. Sweat had run down over his beltless waist. His thighs and legs were wet except where the pants pockets were. He kept rubbing his hands along the sides of his legs.

Bert spoke up, "All I know is, he come on the lot early this mornin', I seen him unhitch his mules and move over there in the shade," pointing in the direction of the clump of pine trees on the edge of the gin yard. "He was waitin' over there most of the day."

"This beats all," Mr. Sapp said, shaking his head as if he was really exasperated. He looked at the men around him, trying to decide what to do. PJ knew exactly what Mr. Sapp was thinking. It wasn't right to just go on ginning Mr. Tom's cotton as if nothing had happened. But there was that other thing. Wagons were backed up out there on the lot. Drivers were sitting around in the shade when they ought to be on their way back to the fields. He had to think about those things too.

In the engine room the pulse of the big motor idled fretfully. The engine would almost die, then start up suddenly and run cleanly for a few seconds as if eager and ready to be at its work. Then it would stumble and almost die again. The big engine called to them. It pleaded with them.

Beryl decided to say something. "I ought to set the idle up on that motor." But he knew and everybody else knew now wasn't the time, and he wasn't one to make such a decision.

PJ could see Cyrus Sapp was trying to figure it out. How do you be respectful to the dead when they have been so disrespectful as to die at the worst possible time? PJ knew that was the problem. That was what was so exasperating.

Mr. Tom was stretched out there in the walkway right where people had to work, his own cotton only half-ginned. And all those trucks and trailers and wagons pulled up out there, waiting.

It was going to be an all-nighter for sure.

Mr. Tom kept lying there, his eyes open, his limp body in a state of comfortable perpetual rest. He was not in any hurry.

PJ knew somebody had to decide.

Speaking softly, Mr. Sapp asked, "Lee Junior, you know this man's family, don't you?"

Junior nodded. He rubbed more sweat off his hands along the sides of his pants.

At least that was something. Mr. Sapp was getting on with it. PJ saw that Mr. Sapp was now looking directly at him. "PJ, you get in the pickup. Take Lee Junior with you. Go over to Arlyn Jones's place and tell Mr. Jones we got a problem over here.

And he turned to Lee Junior and lowered his voice. "You don't let this man's family get all upset, you hear? We don't want a bunch of people running all over the place. OK? Now you two get a move on."

"Yes sir," PJ said, motioning for Lee Junior to follow. He was pleased because they were going to be able to help out. There was real satisfaction in knowing that he was finally one of the men. When you grow up you have to know how to handle situations like these. You've got to take orders and move quick.

PJ was halfway up the steps, but Lee Junior wasn't coming. Lee Junior wanted to come, was trying to come, but couldn't. He couldn't step over the dead man that was in his way.

"Come on, Lee Junior," PJ yelled impatiently.

Mr. Sapp saw Lee Junior's problem and said to him gently, "Son, go on around the other way."

Lee Junior had to jump to catch the door handle and pull himself onto the running board as the pickup came past him. He swung into the cab as the truck, its motor racing and empty gasoline cans rolling loose in the back, spun around the corner of the waiting shed.

PJ noticed a farmer get quickly up from a bench near the drinking water barrel to steady his team, as the truck sped by. A couple of checker players looked up from their game of homemade cardboard and RC and Nehi bottle caps. Somebody taking a nap lifted his straw hat off his face and raised up from his cotton sack pillow to see what was going on. A fine spray of dust from the dry gin yard lifted behind the pickup and filtered across the open shed.

Dodging cotton wagons parked in patient succession, PJ found an opening to the road and raced the truck northward. He sat upright holding onto the steering wheel for height, his legs stretching to reach both clutch and accelerator. The afternoon sun struck him in the face through the open window.

At Beeman's store a hundred yards down the farm-to-market, PJ pulled the truck sharply to the right and gunned it down the sandy surface of the lane heading east. This was the same dirt road that was their shortcut to the River. Lee Junior held stiffly onto the pickup seat as if he were riding a runaway wagon.

Neither said anything. They were concentrating on the road. PJ, thinking about his arrival at the Arlyn Jones place, was rehearsing what he was going to say. But before he knew it, he had passed somebody going in the other direction, a large woman running.

"Dat's Miss Mary," Lee Junior exclaimed, turning in his seat.

"Who?" PJ took his foot off the accelerator.

"Hit's Miss Mary. Miss Tom."

PJ stopped the truck. They both looked back. The dust boiled up over her. She paid no attention to the dust or to the truck.

Her heavy legs were carrying her as fast as they could go in the direction of the store and the cotton gin.

PJ turned the truck around.

Lee Junior spoke to her out the window as the pickup caught up with her. "Miss Mary, you wants a ride?" he said. She was still wearing her apron. Her brown stockings were down around her ankles, flapping loosely as she ran.

"Somethin's happened to Tom," she fretted. "Somethin's happened to Tom."

She was breathing hard. Fear was in her face. She didn't pause but continued to run alongside the truck.

PJ felt goose bumps against his shirt on the undersides of his arms. Lee Junior was paler than he had ever seen him. He had a kind of twitch in his neck muscles that PJ had not seen before.

Miss Mary suddenly paused on the edge of the road. PJ disengaged the clutch and the truck paused with her.

"Why da gin stop?" Miss Mary whined, her broad face pained with the dread. "Tell me, tell me he all right. He all right, ain't he?" Miss Mary had her big hands on the door at the window and was peering in.

Lee Junior started to say, "We was jes goin' out . . ." but he never finished. He heard the sound from the gin starting up.

They all heard it, as everyone for miles around could hear it. The throttle was opening on the engine of the cotton gin. The pistons were firing one after the other. The cams were starting to pull. The clutch was now engaged, which meant that the drive belt had set into motion all those pulleys, augers, rollers, saws and fans, each moving faster and faster until the afternoon air was once again filled with its mighty presence.

"Dey started up the gin?" Junior said, not believing.

Miss Mary must have thought it a miracle, for she looked up and raised her arms to the sky. "Glory be," she said aloud. "Thank ye Jesus."

But as quickly she lowered her hands, and pushed her head into the window. "Dat means Tom's all right?" she demanded.

When she did not see in either of their faces the reassurance she was looking for, she started to cry and began to beat on the cab of the pickup with her fists, demanding, "Hit means he's all right, don't it?"

PJ could not meet her eyes. Instead he looked in the direction of the gin and thought how different the sound of a cotton gin is at a distance than right up close.

He thought about Mr. Sapp, his gold wire glasses, his ironed khaki shirt and how he kept so clean with all the dust floating in the air. He had to do it. PJ was convinced of that. There were those trucks and trailers and wagons on the yard waiting patiently to take their turn, all of them needing to get back to the field, so they could bring more cotton to be ginned. It's what he had to do.

Lee Junior was the one who opened the door on his side and got out. "Miss Mary, its best you just get in. . . .We will takes you on up to the store."

THE SCHOOL

On the wall of the school auditorium, up front near the stage, was a picture of PJ's father, Rayford Purdee, in uniform. It hung in a thin black frame just under the unfinished portrait of George Washington. It had been there a long time.

The auditorium in the three-room schoolhouse also served as the lunchroom. That noon in late November, PJ sat at the end of Principal Dever Dromgould's table, trying to decide who might have put the picture there.

He saw it almost every day, the way one notices the flag, the Declaration of Independence, and George Washington's portrait without really examining them. These few wall decorations all got more concentrated study during long assemblies, as cracks in the ceiling and patterns in wallpaper get observed more closely when one is home sick in bed. That was the way PJ was studying the picture now.

His father's name, his rank and any words of explanation had long since disappeared. A white space marked where a card or nameplate might have been. He thought that whatever it was may have fallen to the floor and been swept out after some national election, for the Prairie community's polling always took place in the school lunchroom.

Today, PJ sat eating his lite bread and navy beans, trying to decide if what he knew about his father was what he himself remembered, or was it only what people had told him.

In his mind, he had two, maybe three, clear remembrances of his father. The earliest, which came to him like something taken out of a movie, was a full-color motion picture of a little boy running into his house. There he found a tall man, dressed in a soldier's uniform, embracing his mother. In this picture, the man turned, reached down and picked the boy up. He hugged him and whirled him around, and, in his excitement and pleasure, threw the boy up and smashed his head into the low ceiling of the living room.

Had that happened? Had he cried and run and hid in the chicken coop? Was it something he did himself remember, or had he only heard it told so many times by Gran Purdee that it seemed it was his own recollection?

From behind the glass, the man who was his father was looking out with bright eyes. One eyebrow was slightly lifted and on his lips a word seemed frozen in place. PJ thought he might have been about to say something. Or wanted to say something still.

"I knew him, you know."

Startled, PJ turned and saw that Mrs. Dromgould stood at his side. She had almost whispered the words, as if they were a secret she was sharing with him alone.

"May I sit?" she asked, easing onto a chair. Jolene Dromgould weighed about 250 pounds. She had been known to break chairs just sitting on them.

PJ was surprised to see that everybody except him had finished their banana pudding, scraped their plates and already gone out to recess. "You knew my daddy?"

She had her little girl's smile. Sometimes Jolene Dromgould looked at PJ as if she were about to eat him. That's the way she looked at that moment. "I should say I did."

PJ had been in Mrs. Dromgould's room for fourth and fifth grades and in Mr. Dromgould's for sixth, seventh, and now eighth grade. Neither one of them had ever mentioned to PJ that they knew his father.

"Both years your father made All-State," she said, as if she were revealing a confidence only the two of them should know about, "I was a cheerleader."

PJ just could not imagine it. Jolene Dromgould, a woman who had her own special lunchroom chair, once wore short skirts and turned cartwheels?

He had been to basketball games. Now that Roy was up at the high school, he had been to two ball games this year. He had seen the Theodosa cheerleaders, showing their black panties, leading the crowd in yells, "Rah Rah, Sis Boom Bah, Tigers, Tigers, Ah Yah Yah." Could Mrs. Dromgould have ever really been one of those girls dressed in black and yellow, leapfrogging over each other, shaking their skinny behinds?

"You don't believe me, do you?"

As strange as it was, he did believe her.

"I was a majorette too. I almost made drum major. When I was just your age - you're 14 now aren't you, PJ? - I got sent to drum major camp in Jackson, Mississippi. I could throw a baton twenty feet in the air and catch it behind my back."

She leaned her heavy arms on the table and looked at the picture for a long time. "I was special then. . . like him. He was very special."

PJ asked if she had played basketball.

She either didn't hear him or had something else on her mind, for she said, "Some of those away games, you know, we didn't get back from until two or three in the morning."

PJ wanted to ask about some of those games but she continued, "Every town the bus went through, we let all the windows down and sang the Tiger Fight Song. Nearly always there was a caravan of cars behind us, sometimes a quarter mile long."

"Just ask your GranPap. He will tell you. He drove one of the buses."

"Did my mother go along on those trips?" PJ asked.

"Of course, she did. Everybody on the girls' basketball team went to the boys' games. Her father was the coach."

"I knew my mother's daddy was the boys' basketball coach. Did he also coach the girls' team?"

"Jim Carr was both the girls' coach and the boys' coach at Theodosa High School. Everybody followed Coach Carr. His players won the most games in the history of our school, and later he was recruited to coach in universities. As you now must know, he just this year made himself even more famous by being hired to coach at the University of Florida."

"Did he and my mother have some kind of falling out?"

Jolene Dromgould looked at him sharply, like he was asking

a question she didn't want to answer. She took a breath, and thought for a full minute before she said, "They did, but I am not going to talk to you about that. You have to find that out from your mother."

PJ wanted to know more. This was a sore subject for his mother. Ever since he was old enough to ask, his mother Belle evaded questions that he and Roy had about their other grandparents. Mostly, she just dismissed the subject, except to say that her dad was too busy coaching basketball to care about them.

For the first time, PJ realized that this was also an untouchable topic for Jolene Dromgould way out here on Sandy Prairie. Why was that? This new information totally confounded him; it was news he needed to mull over and sort out.

If what Jolene Dromgould was telling him was true, it would mean that his mother hadn't told her boys for a reason. Did the Carr family not approve of their daughter Belle marrying Rayford Purdee? Why would that be? Wouldn't their mother's parents want to know that they had two grandsons living less than 30 miles away from Theodosa?

Jolene Domgould clearly wasn't going to say any more about that, for she just kept talking about what a fine basketball team the Theodosa boys were that year when they took State honors.

"They gave it everything they had when they played. You better believe they faced some mean teams. Fast, some of those teams were like acrobats on the court. Some had players so tall all they did was stand in front of our net and bat the balls away. But wasn't anybody could beat our boys. If they were behind, which they were lots of times, we cheered 'em up and cheered 'em on and they won, every time."

"Did my mother. . ."

"You know, PJ," she said, looking right at him, "your brother, Roy, he takes after your mother. You're more like your father. I can tell you that for certain. You are a lot like him."

"I'm not too good a basketball player."

"You will be."

"You think so?"

"I'm just as sure as I can be," she said licking her lips.

"But wasn't my mother real good too, like they say?"

Mrs. Dromgould moved her hand just enough to have it hover over his. "You're going to be a lot like your father Rayford," she said.

PJ didn't know what to make of the way she was acting. "You mean my mother wasn't that good a player?"

"No, Belle was quite good as a player." But the way she said it made PJ doubt whether she really was. Or maybe there was something else entirely.

"Did you see the game where the girls played the boys?" he asked.

She didn't seem to want to discuss it. "I was at the game you're talking about," she said finally. "But, PJ, it wasn't the way they tell it. For the whole first-half our boys were just showing off."

"They weren't really playing, you mean?"

"That's right. They didn't need to, you see. They were unbeatable."

"But the girls beat 'em."

"I told 'em. I told them they were letting the girls get too big a lead. I told them they were going to have to get serious."

"But it was too late?"

"It was too late."

"So they lost it."

"You can be sure they wouldn't have if they'd been playing for real."

"But the girls must've been good too?"

"They were. But they weren't anywhere near as good as the boys. People just remember the final score and not how that game was played."

"It must've come between them," PJ said, thinking how it would be for a girl to best a boy like that.

"What?"

"The score of that game?"

"Who?"

"My father and my mother."

Mrs. Dromgould's hand dropped onto his and squeezed it. "Oh, PJ, that's the other thing people have all forgot. Rayford Purdee never took the slightest notice of any girl but me until after that game. People just remember how it ended up, not how it actually was."

Her skin was all red, as if she had gotten caught in a bunch of stinging nettles. Her eyes were moist with pain. "We were so close, PJ," she said. It was a truth she seemed to need to convince him of. "So close."

PJ stood out by the well house and watched Nubbin Matter pick up at least twenty marbles in a game of keeps.

Mr. Dromgould didn't permit smoking, cursing, or playing for keeps. But Mr. D didn't see and hear much of what went on.

At any recess the teacher, who was also the principal, could be seen walking the borders of the schoolyard like a prisoner.

His hands were clasped behind his back, which made him look as if he were searching for some small thing on the ground. He paced from the outdoor toilets to the churchyard, from the church out to the road, then along the side of the road to the volleyball court, and back out to the toilets again.

Dever Dromgould wore the same clothes every day, a black felt hat with a stiff broad brim and a worn black suit. His hands, his pockets and his coattails were permanently powder white with chalk dust. Sticking out of his back pocket was a black-handled brass bell that he rang vigorously at exactly the same time each day to announce lunch and the beginnings and endings of recess.

Mr. Dromgould was somewhat older than his wife. They had one child, Pat, a mentally retarded boy of 12 who wandered almost unnoticed in and out of the two classrooms of the school.

For four years, the Dromgoulds had occupied the teacherage, an unimportant frame structure sitting so high up on cement blocks you could see under the house and right out the other side. The house, with a single pomegranate bush and no yard, abutted Bert Pixley's cotton patch on the other side of a barbwire fence at the rear of the school.

The Dromgoulds paid no rent and got free milk, additional

benefits the community felt fortunate to be able to provide. Teachers the caliber of Dever Dromgould and his wife were hard to find. Mr. Dromgould, it was said, was a graduate of the University of the South and a published author. His wife, although not apt to run any footraces, was known to have taught children to read who hadn't the sense to get in out of the rain.

PJ thought both of them oddities. Just by the way Mr. Dromgould asked questions, he could show that you knew things you had no idea were in your head. Yet, sometimes he would go through an entire day without abiding a single interruption.

Each day, Mr. Dromgould took his hat, which he held over his heart during Pledge of Allegiance to the Flag, and hung it on the last peg of the coat rack by the door.

He gave assignments in reading and writing and began his lectures. Starting with the eighth graders seated by the wall on his left hand, he addressed each of the three classes one row at a time, finishing with the sixth graders sitting to his right along the windows. This he did all day long, broken by lunch and by recess, according to a predictable routine.

Mr. Dromgould lectured without notes, repeating almost word for word what was in the book. He often recited poems and quoted great men from memory.

Starting before the blackboard, chalk in hand, in the front of the room, he always paced north to south along each row and back again just in time to illustrate his thought in a word or diagram upon the board. He never lost his place or misspoke, though sometimes, approaching the door or the long row of windows along the west, he paused for a full minute or two gazing out.

It was his custom at the conclusion of a lecture to call on class members to answer questions, show their papers or to recite. Anyone, no matter the grade level, might respond to any assignment or any question.

Sometimes he gave encouragement to the sixth and seventh grades by calling on its members to fill in information which only eighth graders would normally have been expected to know.

Since PJ, like most of his classmates, had for the two previous years listened without choice to the same lectures, and often gone ahead and read the same books, he had already done most of the eighth-grade assignments, sometimes twice, and didn't mind.

To be truthful, he had liked this part and appreciated the opportunity, especially when he was in sixth grade, to imagine that at the age of twelve he was capable of the exacting work required of those much older.

But, by the time he was 14, the fascination for eighth-grade health and history and geography had faded. Even when he was paying no attention whatsoever, he could almost always give an answer. He had, in that respect, picked up the habits of his teacher.

Dever Dromgould was not well and therefore was not strong. He had a stomach ulcer for which he had to watch what he ate. He drank a pint of sweet cream three times a day. So when the Swadley boy, who refused to stand for a whipping, jerked the belt out of Mr. Dromgould's hand, it pulled the teacher's arm right out of its socket. Bill Swadley was almost 18 and still in the eighth grade.

PJ remembered Mr. Dromgould blocking the doorway of their classroom, his arm hanging limp at his side, saying, "I am unable restrain you, Bill Swadley, but if you want to be in this school, you will take your punishment like everybody else."

Mr. Dromgould had to get the veterinarian to fix his arm. And even though the Swadleys ran a campaign to get him fired, Mr. Dromgould was able to report in assembly that the school board had stood behind him one hundred per cent. Bill Swadley quit school and went to hauling logs with his brother.

Before he moved up to the high school, up in the county seat at Theodosa, PJ's brother Roy was always in some trouble or another. It was never anything big, but he and Mr. Dromgould seemed to clash. Mostly Roy was just being himself, butting in where he had no business or playing practical jokes on people who would least appreciate them.

Roy was very likely the main reason there were so many unfortunate stories about Mr. Dromgould in circulation about the Prairie.

But only once did PJ ever have any difficulty with his teacher. He remembered that particular incident as one of those moments of true misunderstanding when, once it happens, can only be played out to its painful end.

PJ had put some math problems on the blackboard. When he was called on to explain what he had done, Mr. Dromgould asked him where his decimal points were.

"They're there," PJ told him.

"If they are," his teacher said, "I'd say they're rather faint."

PJ went up, made all the decimal points the size of a silver dollar, and sat down again.

Mr. Dromgould promptly lifted the paddle from its place on the front wall and proceeded to the aisle where PJ was sitting. He must have intended to whap PJ on the side of the leg but he hit the desk instead. It made a noise like a .30.30 rifle shot. "Don't you get smart with me, young man."

Another time, when PJ was popping flies in the lunchroom with his red bandana, Mr. Dromgould came up and put his hand on his arm. "PJ, the proper place for a snot-rag is in your pocket. Germs should be shared only when necessary."

All told, Mr. Dromgould was the gentlest of persons and they got along.

Today, PJ didn't join in with the marble shooters. He didn't take the basketball out to the light pole to practice free throws and jump shots off the backboard. The girls were playing Rover Red Rover but he did not go in that direction. Instead, he walked over into the churchyard and sat under the big pine.

It was now late September. The cotton was almost all in. The gin was mostly silent, running only one or two days a week.

He listened for Lee Junior's tractor, but he didn't hear it.

There were only the log trucks going by on the road, the girls calling "Red Rover, Red Rover, let Darcy come over" and the faint breeze blowing high up in the pine.

A fear was in him. He didn't know what it was exactly. It was in his stomach, and had spread all the way down into his legs, the way it was when he had been bad and was waiting to be punished, or when something he wanted very much was about not to happen.

Yesterday, his mother had done something he never expected. She opened the trunk with all his father's things in it and started giving them away.

PJ now realized it had all started on Thursday of the week before when his grandmother Purdee sent a note asking Belle to come over after work. And, surprisingly, Belle drove over to the big house again on Friday, and stayed past their normal time for supper. It was more than odd that Roy and PJ were not invited to come along.

They could see that Belle was smoldering like a seed house fire, but they did not know the reason. When she got home from the poultry processing plant on Saturday, she was in no kind of mood to be cheered up. They dressed and went to the movies in town as they always did.

Afterward, the boys tried to get her to stop over to the cafe. She wasn't about to, even to get something to go. She would put up with no arguments, listen to no entreaties. Her mouth was set in that hard white line, the way it is when she has made up her mind.

They had heard her crying during the night and the next morning she looked like she hadn't slept at all. Over breakfast she told them, "I won't be going to church this morning. You can go if you want to, but I'm cleaning out that trunk with your Dad's things in it. You two'll have to decide if you want any of it."

She gave his father's high school letter jacket to Roy. "Somebody might as well get some wear out of this," she said. Roy also talked her into letting him have his father's class ring. His mother used to wear that ring around her neck. When she gave it to Roy, it still had running through the band the three plaited strands of yellow, red and black yarn, symbolizing the Tiger colors that brought them together and the love that bound them forever. At least that is what she once had said.

The next morning, when Roy left the house to catch the

school bus that would take him to Theodosa, he was wearing a taped-up ring and a jacket too big for him.

Maybe because of his old asthma affliction, Roy was smaller than his age. On that day, PJ thought his brother looked like one of those girls who hung around high school athletes. PJ could just imagine him strutting down the halls of the high school making a big "to-do" over the fact that his father was once a big Theodosa star.

To PJ, Belle gave the wool sweater, the black one with the yellow trim his father was wearing in his yearbook picture.

He tried it on, because his mother wanted him to, but he put it in his dresser drawer along with his army knife, his shooting taws, his Blue Horse coupons, his luna moth collection and his Illustrated Beowulf. For PJ, his father's school sweater was not something to be worn. It was something to save, to look at, and think about.

From a taped-up cardboard box his mother was going to throw out, PJ retrieved an armful of stuff. When he asked if he could have some of it she told him, "If you want. Have it all. It's just junk. Nobody cares about those things anymore."

At first, PJ was only wanting to retrieve the three-ring binders. He liked the glossy black covers with the small tiger's face embossed in the corner, and he liked the fact that they were made of sturdy material. They would be useful for keeping his pencil drawings, photographs and such.

When he looked further, he realized that his father, like himself, had been a collector, and a very orderly one. The contents of these binders contained things like a program from the Junior-Senior Banquet, on which he had written the names of all those present, an announcement of a school play, some articles his father had written for The Dosa, the school newspaper, clippings about him as a school leader and athlete, and pictures of people PJ did not know.

Roy wanted the trophies and the ribbons. PJ wanted the little parachute. Roy argued for and got the two hand grenades. She let them settle between themselves who would get the fancy uniform with the medals on it. Most of these things they ended up just transferring from their mother's room to theirs.

Their mother told them, somewhat defensively, "Some of that stuff I'd give to Gran, but what's she going to do with it?"

Gran Purdee could find a place for it, PJ knew, every bit of it. Her mantle, the top of her radio, her knickknack shelves, her cupboards, all had some little memorial to her son. But, of course, to walk through GranDee's door with the intention of depositing on her dining room table all the remaining mementos and memories of their father, that would be cruel.

PJ understood that his mother Belle's only real choice was to either pass her husband's things on to Roy and him, or throw them away. What he did not understand was why she was no longer willing to keep them for herself.

Mr. Dromgould paused at the big pine when he came around that way. "PJ, you sick?" he asked.

"No sir."

The teacher still had his hands clasped behind his back. He hadn't even changed the direction he was heading. He just rotated his upper frame from the waist the way a north-east-south-west bug does when you hold it between your thumb and your forefinger. "Having trouble?"

"No sir."

"Just thinking something out?"

"Yes sir."

"You wouldn't hesitate to call on me if I could be of any assistance?"

"No sir."

With that, his teacher turned and paced forward. PJ watched him as he approached the road and walked parallel to it following the eastern edge of the school yard. Across the way, he saw Mr. Beeman lift his hand and wave to Mr. Dromgould from where he stood by the gas pumps in the front of the store. As anticipated, PJ noted the slight nod of the teacher's black hat as his slim frame leaned painfully forward to continue along the dusty path.

From his pants pocket PJ took out the little parachute. He

unfolded the silk from around the cartridge and spread it on the pine straw before him. It'd been seven years. Yes, that's right, he was in the first grade, in Miss Anthony's room, when his father dive–bombed the school.

That at least must've been true, for here was evidence of it.

Everybody ran onto the school grounds. They thought the Germans, or maybe the Japs, had gotten through the lines and were attacking the Sandy Prairie community.

But when they saw it was really an American plane, circling low, tipping its wings, so close they could see the person in it, they waved and cheered. And when the airplane came around again this little silk handkerchief slipped out of its belly and came floating down.

The wind took the homemade parachute and blew it across the road – right about where Mr. Beeman had waved to Mr. Dromgould on the school ground – and it landed on the ice house at the store.

The handkerchief was yellow, the color of pure sulphur, and you could see that something was attached to it.

What it was, was a .50-caliber shell with its powder removed and room enough inside the casing for a message.

Belle had kept the penciled note in a glass frame, along with a picture of her husband and his buddies standing in front of his plane. The note said:

SAY HI TO THAT PRETTY PURDEE GIRL
THAT'S THE CENTER OF THIS MAN'S WORLD
RAYFORD PURDEE

Everybody knew about Rayford Purdee dive-bombing the Sandy Prairie school. That little parachute and its note was one of the things people talked about, in the same way they talked about the big flood when a River-bend couple spent all day and a night in a tree full of water moccasins, or Beryl Forkner's babies getting burned up in the fire, or Guy Stookey going off the Shawnee bridge.

Local people seemed to be full of admiration and pity. Admiration that such a perfect union was made in the marriage of

Belle Carr and Rayford Purdee, and pity that it was cut so short when his father and crew were shot down in their long-range bomber – the Vultee Liberator – off the coast of Portugal in 1944. PJ had heard these sentiments all his life.

Why would his mother not wish to hold such a tragically beautiful thing close to her?

After civics, Mr. Dromgould let PJ take the sixth grade out into the schoolyard to do fractions. PJ now did this quite often. Mr. Dromgould had said several times publicly that his student was better at explaining math than he was. The boy had the talent to make practical what he, as their college-trained teacher, could only visualize as "ethereal magnitudes, quantities, forms and relationships," he said.

It wasn't true, but PJ didn't mind that Mr. Dromgould thought so. He tried hard to live up to the high estimation his teacher had of him.

PJ had heard somewhere, perhaps from his sometimes employer Mr. Sapp, that a man who could do math could just about write his own ticket in the world of business.

That's what PJ tried, in as many ways as he knew how, to show the sixth graders. And not just the boys. In his mind, there wasn't the slightest justification for people thinking women didn't need to learn math. As adults, they would need to know how to convert recipes and dress patterns, or any of the calculations of farm life. As Mr. D would say, it is just a matter of seeing "the forms and the relationships."

Within a week of the opening of school, PJ had taken the class across the road to the store where they went along the grocery shelves deciding if it was cheaper to buy two small cans of green beans at 12 cents or one big one at 25. They even figured out – without telling Mr. Beeman or Mr. Dromgould – the secret code that the store used in putting the purchased price as well as the selling price of each product on the shelf. The key to figuring out what the store paid for the item was to know that the alphabetical letters used represented specific numbers, and number combinations.

The students and he were proud of that discovery, and promised among themselves that they would never tell.

On another day, they were at the gin with a yardstick measuring the capacities of cotton wagons and seed bins. Out on the road, they flagged down Mingus Stump and talked him into waiting while they calculated the number of cords he was hauling on his pulpwood truck. Later, although it took them some time to figure it out, they were able to give Bert Pixley a reasonably accurate estimate of the amount of ground, in square feet, square yards and square rods, he had in chicken houses.

Since Mr. Beeman, Mr. Sapp, Mr. Stump, and Mr. Pixley all happened to have sat on the school board at one time or another, and since, according to Mr. Dromgould, they all happened to think very highly of the idea of "practical fieldwork," his star pupil was given considerable freedom with eight sixth graders.

According to reports of the meeting, Mr. Pixley pretty well summed it up. He had said, "It's not going to be too long before those of us on the Board are going to have to go back to school to keep up with young PJ."

"Mr. Purdee, we await your report," Mr. Dromgould always said when PJ brought his class back precisely at 3 o'clock.

The teacher's assistant didn't always get to give his report, for sometimes the students were so pleased with themselves, so determined to show that they could learn on their own, they shouted him down. "Let us tell it, PJ," they insisted. And five of them were girls.

There were those times when the pupils didn't know how to figure something out, like the amount of water in the cistern or the number of board feet in the big pine, when Mr. Dromgould took to the blackboard and got everybody, seventh and eighth graders included, thinking about how a solution might be found.

These were among the few instances Mr. Dromgould's forward-leaning posture straightened and the number of complete rounds he made from front to back of the classroom was considerably abbreviated.

But there were also times when it seemed that all the sixth

grade wanted to do was to make math class into another recess. They forgot that the opportunity to go outside to do math problems was as easily taken away as it was given. It caused PJ considerable worry, especially about what would happen the day the class returned with nothing at all to report.

Today could be that day. Class members were running off in four different directions. His mind wasn't very well fixed on fractions. He hadn't really been able to think about where he should take them and what he wanted them to do. His pupils weren't waiting around for him to come up with something.

"I'm not goin' to chase you all over the place," he yelled after Andy Burdeen and Abby Silver, who were way over in the churchyard.

PJ appealed to them, "What're you goin' to report about fractions if you haven't measured anything?" He dreaded going in with nothing. It looked like that was the way it was going to be.

"I'm afraid we didn't accomplish very much today, sir."

"So you have no report?"

"No sir."

"Having some discipline problems, PJ?"

I guess so, sir. It's not their fault though," he quickly added.

"The responsibility is yours, is that it?"

"Yes sir. I just hadn't thought enough about what I wanted 'em to do."

"We'll see," he replied and said no more about it.

PJ went straight home after school. He pulled his father's notebooks from under his bed. He turned each page and fingered each yellowing clipping and searched each faded photograph as if he were peeling back layers of history that happened just before his time.

Around four o'clock Roy came in with Itchy Gates in tow. "PJ, old buddy, would you mind finding someplace else to do that. Itchy and me want to listen to records."

PJ did not protest. Sometimes he would assert his rights. Today he took the notebooks and went out and sat under the chinaberry tree.

He must have been there for over an hour for suddenly he was aware it was time for his mother to be coming in from the plant. He dashed into the house but found the door to his and Roy's room locked.

"Roy, you let me in."

"What you want, PJ?" Roy sounded far away like he was under the bed or behind some clothes in the closet.

"I want in."

"Later."

"Come on, Roy. I need in."

"Not now, brother."

PJ turned and went out onto the back porch. He left the notebooks in an egg basket and ran all the way to the store. He wanted to be there when his mother got dropped off from her car pool.

He was regretting all the times he had missed meeting her and hoped that she would today have a smile for him and a hug for Mr. Beeman. It would mean that she was feeling better. If she stopped in at the store and kidded around with Mr. Beeman, that would mean that things were still more the way they were.

PJ was the first one at school the next morning. He was sitting on the steps when Mr. Dromgould arrived. "Well, well. Thirsting after knowledge, are we young man?"

"No sir. I just thought I'd help Mrs. D sweep up before school."

"That's thoughtful."

With his skeleton key, Mr. Dromgould unlocked the lunchroom door and the doors of each of the classrooms. From a barrel in the broom closet he dipped a can full of oiled sawdust and gave it to PJ. "This helps to get the grit up," he said. "Watch there are no books or papers on the floor. You can wet a rag at the cistern and clean the boards if you have time."

By the time Mrs. Dromgould arrived, PJ had raised the windows, swept out, wiped the blackboards, rearranged the children's encyclopedias in the shelves and was about to dust the erasers.

Mrs. Dromgould's room always seemed so light and cheery. Bright pictures of baby baboons making faces and volcanoes erupting, bowls of fresh fruit and heaping plates of muffins fresh out of the oven decorated the walls.

"My goodness, aren't you sweet." Mrs. Dromgould was completely out of breath and holding onto the door frame after her walk over from the teacherage and climb up the steps. "Look at you. You've made everything look so nice."

At the front of the room was a large wooden chair on rollers. This was the way Mrs. Dromgould moved about the classroom. She let herself down into her chair with a heavy sigh. "I don't know what I've done to deserve such a nice present from you today."

PJ looked to see if they were alone. From the front pocket of his bib overalls he took a small photograph. He went up to Jolene Dromgould and handed it to her. She took it and looked at it and then looked at him and again at the picture.

"Oh my," she said, shaking her head. "Oh my."

THE CROSSROADS STORE

On an afternoon in early December, PJ was inside the Crossroads store waiting for his mother.

Working the 7AM to 4PM shift at the poultry plant in Theodosa, Belle Purdee normally arrived back on the Prairie around five o'clock in the afternoon.

PJ had brought her a warm sweater and a rain slicker for the walk home. Since noon, it had turned off cold. Now it was raining hard, and the rain was turning to sleet. But the weather wasn't the real reason he wanted to be at the store that afternoon.

The soil conservation man was in the store buying a loaf of bread and a piece of candy. It was a Mounds bar he had chosen, one of PJ's favorites, but he thought it cost too much. Mr. Beeman was ringing up the sale on the cash register. The man's heavy coat hung open. Water from his shoes darkened the pine flooring in a puddle where he stood.

Mr. Beeman came around from behind the counter. He put the bread and candy into a bag and gave the man his change. "PJ, let me get in there," he said.

PJ slid off the soda water box where he was sitting. The store proprietor opened the lid and began searching around for a Strawberry Cream. The cold drinks in the box were half-hidden in ice water. It struck PJ as funny that Mr. Beeman was using good icehouse ice to keep his soda pops cold when it was raining sleet outside.

PJ watched him move all the Royal Crown Colas over to the side, then sort out the Nehi grapes and oranges. Where his hands and arms got wet, the hair was straight and black. Above the wet, the hair was red and curly.

"Now don't tell me there ain't no Strawberries," he said as if speaking to himself. Mr. Beeman was a Strawberry-aholic. Drinking Strawberry Cream soda was what you thought of when you thought of Mr. Beeman, the way dipping Red Rooster snuff made you think of the Brown sisters. His brother Roy was the one who first observed that and gave it a name. And PJ thought at the time: "How true that is!"

Mr. Bee may not have really been all that partial to Strawberry Creams, except that somewhere along the way people made that association in their minds. Like Mr. Sapp's Brahmas, Store Manager Beeman is now branded.

After that, Mr. Bee's hands were tied. He had to drink that brand as a matter of loyalty, a matter of consistency, a matter of not wanting to disappoint people who had that idea about him.

"Son-of-a-gun. I let myself run out of Strawberry Creams." Mr. Beeman's rose-red face fell slack like an empty potato sack, almost more than was called for. "PJ, how about putting some more of those Strawberries in here for me, will you? And some Dr. Peppers?"

Mr. Beeman opened a Delaware Punch for himself. As far as PJ was concerned, Delaware Punch was the best soda water made. He rarely drank one, though, because they were only six ounces. For the same nickel you could get a twelve-ounce RC, which wasn't as good but it filled you up and lasted longer.

Thinking about it, PJ assured himself, it wouldn't bother me if he drank something else. If I was him, I would appreciate a change. Sometimes people don't feel comfortable changing over on things like that. But PJ couldn't help wondering whether it had been really an accident that the box had been let run empty of Strawberry Creams.

The soil conservation man looked doubtfully out at the weather. "Say, could I use the phone?"

"Over there on the wall. One long ring gets the operator." Mr. Beeman said and he went and got the mop.

PJ went and got a mixed crate of soft drinks from the back of the store, mostly of NuGrape and Dr. Pepper, and balanced it on the edge of the soda water box while he stood the bottles one by one in the cold water. He decided to rearrange them so that the tall ones like the RCs and Pepsi Colas were to the side, and the smaller ones like the Cokes and the Cream Sodas were more to the middle.

The government man was yelling into the phone. "Sonny is that you? Is Momma home?" There was a pause. "Momma? Earl. I am getting bread down here. I'm coming on home before the weather gets bad out. You need anything else?"

PJ could see Mr. Beeman was trying to keep the conversation going about Joe Truehaw, even though the man was ready to leave. "Just look at his place," Mr. Beeman was saying. "That fellow can't even take his own advice."

PJ didn't know why Bee couldn't just let Joe be who he was.

The message going around Sandy Prairie was that Joe Truehaw was smart, but he hadn't got a lick of common sense. Why would people say that? PJ was beginning to understand that people were getting their ideas about his friend Joe from the store manager, and that information was rarely flattering and it wasn't always accurate either.

Why is it that he doesn't want to give the man the credit he deserves? Mr. Beeman makes Joe seem much less capable than he really is. This bothered PJ because he had a high opinion of Mr. Bee and also of Joe Truehaw, but for entirely different reasons.

The proof that Joe was smart was right there in the Brahma Breeding Station, with its dipping vat and squeeze chute. And in the advice Joe gave to Phil Pharris recommending that he try growing sweet sorghum silage to feed his beef cattle. Those contributions to the community were well-known and talked about.

For two years, Joe had been helping Lee Junior Johnson figure out the varieties of vegetables his family should grow for the Theodosa Farmer's Market, and the fertilizer and lime he should use to augment his soil. He encouraged local farmers to diversify their crops, to grow more than just peanuts and cotton, whose prices he said were likely to continue to be low. All that advice was given for free.

When PJ asked Joe Truehaw about it, he said he wasn't worried about people's opinion. "Sure, it is hard for anybody to change what they are used to doing. Nobody on the Prairie knows anything about growing sweet corn. But as soon as somebody starts, there will be buyers - including you and me."

He said the same thing about planting pecan trees as a commercial crop. "Not everybody can afford to wait that long. And there is a lot of risk entering a market that is not yet proven."

PJ thought it might be ideas like these that gave Joe Truehaw a reputation for not having good judgment.

Mr. Beeman set his Delaware Punch down and with both hands pulled his pants up over the sagging part of his middle. "Now that Joey Lou. She is a go-getter. She's the kind of hand you need around a farm. My guess is, she's put up with just about as much of her daddy's piddlin' as she can stand."

Joe's daughter Joey Lou was a person PJ had come to admire as well. She was only three years older than he was, but she walked and talked just like a man and worked just as hard.

Because she cut her hair short, a stranger would have hardly been able to tell the difference, and that was just fine with Joey Lou.

Nearly everybody had heard the story told on Joey Lou about the time the John Deere man came to fix a hay baler on Mr. Sapp's Low Creek farm. Melvin Aston, Artis Pixley, Lee Junior, Roy, PJ and Joey Lou were all there in the field that day helping to put up hay, when this town mechanic retrieved his tools from the back of his pickup and started working on the baler.

Since all other work was stopped, they gathered around to watch. His brother Roy got the man going on telling farmer's daughter jokes. The visiting mechanic understood that he had an appreciative all-male audience.

Just before he started in on a particularly unacceptable joke, the John Deere man made a point of looking all around as if to be sure there weren't any women in earshot. Then he told his joke and everybody broke down into total hysterics, a lot more than the joke should have merited.

The visiting mechanic looked right at Joey Lou and never had the slightest idea she was a girl. Joey Lou laughed at the joke with the rest and nobody told that man any different.

Joey Lou was like that. She preferred the presence of men. She couldn't imagine choosing housework or any job where you had to be inside. And she herself made jokes PJ would never have thought of re-telling.

For some reason, though, she seemed to single PJ out to pick on. When he was in sixth grade, she used to get him in a head-hold at recess. It was embarrassing the way she dragged him around the schoolyard all bent over, his head tucked up against her side.

But PJ never minded that much. He liked the way she smelled.

Mr. Bee was still going on about the failings of Joe Truehaw. "He won't do it, but he'd be a whole lot better off to slap something up temporary on that barn. That'd keep this rain off of Joey Lou's corn,"

The store manager had followed the soil conservation man over to the entrance to the store. The two of them stood looking out the big front windows toward the road. The lights of the store sparkled on the cab of the government pickup parked close up against the gas stand.

"Of course, it won't make any difference," Mr. Bee said, "They're not going to get their corn out of the field anyway. Last year, he piddled around so long trying to get 10-year old equipment to work that his daughter Joey Lou just gave up. Good corn was left in the field. He's got his priorities all mixed up."

PJ had to admit that Joe Truehaw was not like other people. The first thing PJ had noticed about him was that the man didn't wear a hat. A hat would be a logical way to keep his hair from falling down over his eyes, saving him the effort of having to shove it up every half-minute.

In his face and in his posture, Joe Truehaw reminded PJ of Will Rogers, only he didn't have the comedian's sense of humor. Joe leaned to the serious side. When he saw things in the community that needed to be put right, he felt called upon to say so. This was unfortunate, because his hard positions made people uncomfortable.

He was peculiar in other ways. Joe never referred to himself as a farmer. He used the term "steward of the land" and what he did on his farm he called "stewardship." In some ways, he sounded like a preacher – a man with a calling but no congregation. This calling was particularly true when it came to farming practices that might help keep the fine Prairie topsoil from ending up in the creek.

There was a time when PJ thought his mother Belle was going to get interested in Joe. He was single and nice-looking. He was about the right age. He and his daughter Joey Lou, who was 15-years old at the time, ate off of real tablecloths at home. This impressed his mother.

And Joe liked to ride, as she did. He had a high-headed red mare named Target that he rode in the Sheriff's County Cuadrille. Joe bought and cared for a second horse just for Belle to ride.

On several Sundays, they went out riding on roads through the Cutover and down as far as the River. Once, they went to hear Roy Acuff in person at the Houston Fat Stock Show. They went on the train and stayed for the weekend.

But Belle and Joe started seeing less of each other when Joe took on Kembley and Kembley.

By the time Joe arrived on the Sandy Prairie, most of the native pine in Theodosa County had been gone for twenty years or more. The only virgin forest left was on Indian reservation land on the other side of the River. The Rural Electrification Administration of the United States government had given permission to the lumber company to cut and remove a hundred-yard-wide swath of virgin longleaf pine right down the middle of the Alabama Coushatta reservation, as a first-step in providing the Indians with electric lights.

The next day after the lumber company moved in there, the loggers found their skidder tires punctured and their fuel tanks full of sand. That's when Joe and everybody else was looking at his picture in the newspaper, with him standing on the side of the Indians who were protesting this incursion on reservation land.

Getting involved in Indian affairs didn't sit well with Belle. When she heard the local gossip that "our so-called Native Americans" were sleeping underneath the houses the US Government had built for them, she took the Government side. "For Christ sake, its 1948. They need electricity. Wouldn't you think?"

Joe Truehaw took the position that it was up to the Indian Council to decide whether they wanted electricity or not, and he was quoted in the Theodosa Free Press accusing Kembley and Kembley of "going hell-bent to cut one of the few remaining stands of virgin longleaf pine we have left in the South."

The paper reported him saying, "If you take the forest away, you destroy the place where these people live."

That got PJ's attention. Thereafter, whenever Joe Truehaw had something to say, PJ listened. He thought a lot about Joe's "stewardship" idea. He knew the word from Sunday School, but Joe had used it in the context of his own farm.

"I don't own this land," Joe once said about his farm. "The way I feel about it, the land owns itself. It is just temporarily entrusted to us. The question is, "Will it be worth anything when you and I are gone? Will there be enough topsoil left to grow a tree if somebody decides to plant one?"

Joe was not like other farmers PJ knew. He consulted books and sought the advice of universities. He spent time with the Soil Conservation Service at the County Seat. In a letter published in the Free Press, he had quoted an estimated number of tons of topsoil, an unbelievable amount, that he said was eroding from cotton and peanut farms in Theodosa County each year.

Without radical changes in agricultural practice—leading to State-wide efforts to conserve the soil—he was predicting that in ten years there wouldn't be a farm in the County that could produce a half-bale of cotton an acre.

PJ had heard him say exactly that one day when he was in the store: that "No amount of commercial fertilizer will be able to replace the topsoil in the field where that cotton has to grow."

Store Manager Bee Beeman, who sold fertilizer, did not appreciate the statement at all.

Once PJ had a chance to think about such a dire prediction, it began to make sense to him. He realized the truth of it when he walked down freshly plowed rows in the cotton and peanut fields of the Prairie after a big rain. Topsoil was flowing right out of the field and into the creek. He understood why Joe had said, "Our soil is never coming back; water doesn't flow upstream."

When the two of them had talked about that situation later, Joe had smiled when he said, "There are just not enough of us who are thinking ahead, PJ."

PJ was flattered to know that he had been accepted into Joe Truehaw's congregation.

Only this year had he come to really appreciate the basic principles Joe stood for. But, aside from Cyrus Sapp, hardly anybody else took the man seriously. And here was Mr. Beeman at the store outright ridiculing him to his customers.

As if to keep the conversation with the soil conservation agent going, Mr. Bee asked him directly: "Joe and his daughter Joey Lou didn't hardly get any peanuts from that little patch they planted last year, did they?"

He didn't wait for an answer. "They tell me the hogs were thick as watermelon seed in there. Truehaw could've patched up that old fence. It would've shut out some of 'em, don't you think?"

The soils man agreed. "True, you have to build fence. But I can reassure you that he's laying out a good sturdy fence now." He shifted his bag to his other arm and looked at his pocket watch. "There's nothing wrong with doing things right," he said.

PJ didn't feel easy about Mr. Bee raising that question about the fence, because he knew he was the one who told the store manager about the hogs that were coming into the Truehaw peanut crop at night. PJ had to remind himself: I have to be more careful in what I say around Mr. Beeman.

A car with its lights on pulled off the road and paused opposite the store. It was now raining hard outside. From the warmth of the store, the two men and PJ watched Belle get out of the back seat and come running in the direction of the store.

151

"Well I gotta' go," the soil conservation man said. "Don't be too hard on the Truehaws," he said, smiling. He handed his empty Coca-Cola bottle to Mr. Beeman. "They'll have a nice place out there someday, you'll see."

"If I live long enough to see it," Mr. Beeman said, returning the smile as he let him out the door. The grocer had already turned his attention to the woman coming up the steps.

Belle Purdee held a brown paper bundle above her head the way she might have held a basketball when about to make a jump shot.

"Get in here, Belle," Mr. Bee said, holding the door open for her. "Rain'll melt a pretty thing like you."

PJ's mother freed one hand and pushed at her hair piled high on her head. Long curls had come dislodged and bounced as she moved. He saw that she was wearing what looked like a new dress under a definitely new short coat. The dress had pink flowers and the coat was red.

"What a mess," Belle said, somewhat out of breath. "Did I get my hair all wet, Bee?" She tilted her head to one side so Mr. Beeman could inspect her. "First permanent I've had since I don't know when. And look. I've already got it all wet."

"I never saw anything so beautiful in my whole life," Mr. Beeman said, teasing her. "You know I like your hair down, Belle. You look so good with your hair long. I don't know why you don't wear it down."

"Christ a'mighty, Bee. You don't know anything," Belle scolded him. "Can you imagine what a mess that would be cuttin' up chickens all day long with your hair going everywhere?"

She toyed with him as she handed him the paper bundle. "But sometime I'll let it down just for you. I brought you a present," she said. She grinned at PJ.

Mr. Beeman was obviously pleased. "What you bring me?" he asked, trying to feel it through the paper.

"Gizzards."

"Gizzards?"

"Don't you like gizzards, Bee?" she said, pretending hurt. "I thought that was one of your favorites. The other night at church you was admiring my gizzards."

"Well, yeah. I like gizzards. But Belle, I like 'em when you fix 'em. What am I goin' to do with two pounds of raw gizzards?"

"Don't say I never gave you anything," she kidded him.

To PJ she asked, "Rained you out, did it?"

He nodded, "I guess so." Belle already knew that PJ had planned to help Joey Lou pull corn after school. PJ had even started in that direction but changed his mind and went to the store instead.

PJ knew it might look like he just didn't want to work in the rain. He also knew he wouldn't be able to explain to Joey Lou why he didn't show up when she really needed him. But he just felt he needed to be with his mother.

What he didn't dare say in front of Mr. Beeman was that Joe Truehaw's old horse-drawn corn picker was in multiple pieces laid out under his wagon shed, where it had been since Joe started working on it in August. The Truehaws were not going to have a mechanical picker to help them get this year's crop out of the field.

He had noted that Joey Lou was getting more and more exasperated. The closer to winter it got, the madder she was at her father. By December, the two of them were left with no choice but to pick the field by hand. "He's still determined to fix that piece of junk," she told PJ, "but it isn't happening."

"We'll be out there every night 'til midnight and we still won't have all our corn in. We ought to borrow a corn picker," she said. "Pootie has offered to loan me his, but Dad doesn't want to be indebted to anybody."

Just as an estimation, she had asked PJ to help her figure out how long it would take if she had to do it herself by hand. The two of them calculated that: a) if there were fifty wagonloads of corn in the field to be picked and b) if after school she could herself pull at least one load of ear corn a day, and c) on weekends she could pull two, she could have most of the crop in the crib by the first of January.

She told PJ, "If that's what has to be done, that's what I am going to do. Want to help me?" Of course, they both knew she was kidding. If the rain turned to sleet, and the sleet turned to ice, the weight would ride the corn stalks to the ground.

"Who'd work out in weather like this?" his mother said, shaking her head. "But Joey Lou's probably out there in it, isn't she?"

"She wants to get it done," PJ agreed.

He was hoping Mr. Beeman wouldn't figure out that Joey Lou was intending to pull the Truehaws' corn by-hand. He knew the store manager would spread that story all over the county.

"Is Roy at home?"

"I don't know where he's at," PJ told her, trying not to tell a direct lie. Since Roy and Itchy Gates had found each other, they were spending most afternoons in the boys' room at the house, but he wasn't sure they would still be there.

"Well I hope he straightened the house up. I am in the mind to have a nice dinner tonight."

Belle smiled sweetly at Mr. Beeman. "Bee, Honey, have you got some wine?"

"Belle, you know this is a dry county and I am not allowed to sell wine."

"I didn't ask you if you sold it. I asked if you had any."

"What'll you give me?"

"I just gave you two pounds of gizzards," she teased.

Mr. Beeman laughed. He went back of the counter and from a locked cabinet took a bottle of red wine that had a picture of a game rooster on it. He put the bottle in a paper bag and handed it to her.

"How much is it?"

"I'm not goin' to take your money, Belle."

"You sure as hell will. How much is it?"

"That's a dollar."

"You're not shorten'n yourself now."

"Nah, that'll do."

"You're a nice feller, Bee." She said as she searched around in her purse for money. She took out a dollar bill and gave Mr.

Beeman a quick hug. "You know what I did?"

"No, what did you do?

"I quit my job today. I'm done. Today was my last day at work."

"Belle, you didn't. What are you going to do?"

"Well, tonight, the boys and me are going to have a sit down dinner with candle light.

And tomorrow morning I am going to sleep in as long as I want to."

"I'd invite you over for supper but I know Florine wouldn't come and it wouldn't look right you coming by yourself."

THE INVITATION

As they had done so many times before, PJ and his Mom were walking the half-mile from the store to their rental house across the road from the Dominey pasture.

It was raining and the rain was tuning to ice. Their feet were getting cold. But on this evening, none of that mattered. What mattered was that the mother had quit her job, and that she and her son had a lot to think about.

Belle spoke first, and PJ was surprised by what she said. "I want to invite the Truehaws for dinner."

"Tonight you mean?"

"Yes, especially tonight. I want us to have company for supper. I want people I care about to be here with us, to drink a glass of wine. I want to get out the old Victrola and listen to records. I want us to get up and dance and not think about tomorrow or next week or next month."

What she was saying was totally unexpected. But, who was he to question it? His mother had just quit a job she had held for more than 10 years. If that is what a mother wanted to do when she had just turned their family's life upside down, what could he say?

They didn't slow their fast pace of walking at all, but after a few minutes of not talking, PJ said, "Mom, you know Joe and Joey Lou may still be out there in the field picking their corn."

"I don't care if they are at home sipping mint juleps. I don't want us to be alone tonight. I want you to go over there and tell them they have to come. Tell them Roy's got a roast on and we are going to have a sit-down dinner tonight. Tell them I want them to come."

As they arrived at the front entrance of their house, Belle

paused for a moment, as if she had forgotten something. She then turned and went to their family's mailbox, which was set on a post across the road. PJ saw her reach in and take out an envelope that she looked at briefly but did not open. It was in her hand as they came up on the porch. The two of them shed their wet things and went inside.

Roy had the gas heater turned on, and PJ noticed how it made the house warm and inviting. Glancing around, it looked like Roy may have straightened up the living room and given the kitchen a good cleaning. He had already started to set the table.

PJ was surprised to see the roast, raw red, still sitting out on the counter. Roy was supposed to be preparing them a meal, so why hadn't he started cooking the meat?

PJ's anger was rising, and he was about to say something to Roy, but his mother stood between them and said quite firmly, "Go on now. You go tell the Truehaws that we want them to come. Go right now. Don't accept 'No' for an answer, even if they have already eaten. . . . And, one more thing, you tell Joey Lou that I am expecting her to wear a dress."

Walking on the road would have been an easier way for PJ to get to the Truehaw place, but he knew that going by the road was further. It would take longer. At the end of their lane, PJ climbed the fence and cut straight across the pasture. He followed the cow tracks through the goat weeds and made his way down alongside the creek.

The cardboard box he had picked up on their front porch, thinking he would hold it over his head to keep the rain off, was soon soaking wet and coming apart. When he found the creek too high to cross, he realized he had made a mistake. He threw away the box and went back to the road, heading south in a sloggy run toward the iron bridge.

PJ wasn't sure whether the Truehaws would still be out pulling corn or whether they would have already gone in for the night. Since the cornfield was nearest, he decided he would check there first.

He smiled at the idea of Joey Lou wearing a dress. Nobody

had ever seen Joey Lou in a dress. It wouldn't be Joey Lou. But Belle had said, "You tell her she's to come and she's to wear a dress."

Once on the road, PJ was able to pick up the pace and make better time running. His light jacket had soaked through. His khaki pants stuck to his legs. He could feel the water squishing between his toes in the high-top rubber boots he had put on at the house.

Ahead, he could see the fence line that marked where the Truehaws' cornfield was. It was getting so dark and it was sleeting so hard that he very much doubted Joey Lou would still be out there in the field. It occurred to him that she might not have gone there at all.

He left the road and looked for an easy way to get over the fence. Anybody would have been able to tell that this was a Truehaw fence. The corner posts were creosote with oak cross-supports bolted into place. Each post from the corner on was made from either black locust or bow'darc trees, wood that is harder to find these days but they do have a reputation for never rotting. The old fences, many of them still standing, had been made of longleaf pine, but posts made of longleaf were no longer available.

The fence line was positioned in a perfectly straight row, all post installed at the exact same height, with new hog wire stretched taut on the bottom and two strands of barbed wire stretched straight across the top. Where the ground rose and fell, a Truehaw fence did not. Except when it went down into and up out of the creek, it stayed perfectly level to the eye.

PJ knew from working with him on his place, Joe was hard to please when it came to fencing. He liked a straight fence, he liked a sturdy fence, one that would last, and he liked a clean fence row. He didn't want weeds or any briars growing up in his fence. And he probably wouldn't like me climbing up on it and stretching it out either, PJ thought, as he climbed over to the other side.

PJ remembered when that bunch of guys at the store, who gathered round the wood stove when it was too cold to do anything else, had set out to convince Joe his fence was put in crooked.

They all had such a laugh when Joe fell for it and went back out to his pasture and re-set post he had spent so much time lining up in the first place. None of those posts could have been more than a hair off one way or the other.

PJ had a little chuckle just for himself recalling the event. But he also knew that Joe was particular that way. Those guys could count on that and play on it, as a way to have some fun and embarrass him.

PJ entered the tall corn reluctantly. It was getting darker. The cold leaves slapped and cut at him as he sought to hurry on through. Mud began to hang onto the bottoms of his boots, so that the tracks he made behind him looked like an elephant had come down that corn row.

He recalled that two years ago, when everybody else had their ground all broke and ready for planting, Joe was still hauling chicken manure to put on his fields. He must have put it on at least an inch thick and it made a noticeable difference. But it was a mistake, PJ told himself, to let it be known that he expected to get a hundred bushels of corn per acre off that crop.

His corn crop turned out to be good and he might have done it, but that's when the hogs came in and ruined more than half of the yield because he hadn't finished his fence. Now those kidders at the store are going to get to laugh some more because here he's got a good crop of ear corn and he'll lose most of it because he's left with no way but by-hand to pick it, and his corn crib doesn't yet have a roof on it.

If he would just borrow the money like everybody else he could get some good equipment to work with. Or at least he could ask for help around the Prairie. Pootie Wilson already has his corn in the barn, PJ knew. There would be no shame in asking Pootie to let him use his like-new John Deere corn picker. Pootie was a helping person. He might even operate the picker for him.

Joe makes it worse on himself, he thought. He draws the line too hard and people take it wrong. His mother Belle was right on that point. Back then, she told Mr. Beeman at the store: "The Truehaws would get along better if they would just call time out and send in some replacements every once in a while. There are people on this Prairie who will be more than willing to pitch in and help, rather than see the hogs ruin his crop," she said. "But he will not do that."

PJ heard the corn pullers before he saw them. He paused to be certain. In the heavy stillness, Joe's voice rose above the field and hovered briefly in the damp air, "Up, Ben." Then PJ heard the creaking of the wagon and the breaking of the dried corn stalks as the horses strained forward. PJ listened for the "Whoa."

He came out into the open too far down and had to walk back toward the pickers and their team. In the dark, he could barely see the horses half-hidden in the standing rows of corn, the stalks bowing and falling behind them under the wagon's weight.

Then he saw through the tall corn Joe and his daughter working alongside, breaking the ears away from the stalk, twisting off the shucks and tossing the corn up over the sides into the wagon bed.

Without saying anything, PJ moved into place and started reaching and breaking the ears and pitching them into the wagon as he walked forward with the team. He quickly learned that even though the outer leaves were soaked, the ears on the inside were dry and crisp. They snapped cleanly away from the shuck.

"PJ . . . you didn't have to come out here in this weather," Joe Truehaw said as if surprised to see him.

"My man!" Joey Lou spoke up in a commanding voice. He could tell she was pleased.

PJ kept pace trying to work as fast as they did. When Joey Lou came by him, he spoke quietly to her, "I would've come to help after school but I had something I had to do."

"Don't worry about it," she said.

"Git up there, fella," Joe called. Old Ben shook in his harness like a dog shaking water. Together, Old Ben and the mate horse strained in their leather harness. The wagon groaned. The corn stalks popped and scraped under the belly of the wagon, sounding like an out-of-tune fiddle.

It wasn't until they had worked to the end of the row that PJ said, "I'm supposed to tell you to come to supper."

"Belle wants us to come over?" Joe asked.

"Is that tonight, she means?" Joey Lou wanted to know.

"Soon as you can," PJ said. "She's got a roast on."

"That's real nice, PJ," Joe said. "Are you sure that isn't too much bother?"

"She knew you would say that," PJ said with a smile, "and I am instructed not to take no for an answer. Even if you have already eaten, you are still expected to come."

"Sounds good to me," Joey Lou said. It sounded like she was already thinking about pulling up to the table.

"There's one thing though," he said to Joey Lou, "You have to wear a dress."

"Aw, man," Joey Lou said, a disappointed look coming over her face. "Really?" She suddenly seemed to have lost her appetite.

"That'll be the day," Joe laughed.

"Our mom's got something to celebrate. We're going to have a set-down dinner tonight and she's serving wine."

Joe was concerned. "What's happened?"

"She quit work."

The three of them stood listening to the low roar of the rain hitting the dried corn stalks, a hundred million little splatters merged into a single continuous sound like that of a train going through a tunnel. The horses shifted their weight nervously and snorted, blowing the water from their nostrils.

Joey Lou took off her cap. With a swift downward motion she slung the water out of it and lifted both hands to her head, brushing her wet hair back from her face. Rainwater collected on her eyebrows, and with the turning of her head, the moisture ran in rivulets across her cheeks, disappearing into the collar of her plaid shirt.

"Let's go in then," she said.

Joe spoke to the horses. "Let's go home now."

"We'll unload this one tomorrow," Joe said, backing the wagon into the shed. PJ helped unhitch the team, and, while Joe and Joey Lou went into the house, he led the two horses out to the lot.

Joe's new lot fence was high enough and strong enough even a Brahma bull would be unlikely to escape it. The gate was so perfectly balanced it opened with one hand and swung shut with no effort at all when PJ went through.

The site where the barn had burned to the ground had been raked clean and planted in rye. The sandstone foundations that Joe had not used for his corncrib had been removed and they were stacked neatly against the big black sycamore that, even at 140 feet away, had died from the heat of the fire.

In the light of a 25-watt electric bulb in the harness room of the wagon shed, PJ found a barrel marked Horse and Mule Feed, one marked Shelled Corn, one marked Cracked Corn and one marked Crushed Cob. He filled a dishpan half with the sweet feed and half with crushed corn. This he mixed with his hand and took out to the lot for the horses.

He lingered there, watching them eat.

No farmers he knew cracked their corn for horses. Some did shell corn for their horses but most people just gave them the whole ear to wallow around in their mouths. Joe had told him, "If you shell the corn and crack it, they don't waste as much, and they digest it better."

He had suggested to PJ that he should pay attention to horse manure. "You'll see how much whole corn shows up in that manner."

PJ did start noticing and he saw that Joe was right.

Nobody PJ knew ground up their corn cobs for cow feed. "Cows have a second stomach," Joe had said. "To convert what they eat efficiently, they need a lot of roughage. Ground-up corn cobs are good roughage, but you can use ground-up cotton burrs or sawdust just as well or, if you had a good way to do it, you could re-feed them their own manure."

162

This, PJ was skeptical about. He thought it more likely that Joe had come up with these ideas because he didn't like all the corn cobs and manure left lying around, messing up an otherwise clean-looking barn lot.

He carried the dishpan back and put it in the harness room. Looking for something to use as a chair, he straddled the tongue of the wagon and sat waiting for the Truehaws to come out of the house.

From where he sat he could see the silhouette of the unfinished corncrib. As they picked it, the Truehaws had been loading their ear corn into the new crib, but it still didn't have a roof on it. The trusses were up and the nailing boards were in place, wet black against the night sky, awaiting the installation of the slate.

Slate was something new to PJ. Joe had said it was worth the extra expense. "A good roof makes a barn," he had said, "and slate practically lasts forever." He had acquired some old-time slate from when he helped to take down the County Barn at the fairgrounds in Theodosa, but there wasn't enough of it that was unbroken for him to finish the job.

Later, his new friend Joe sounded apologetic when he told PJ, "The slates are still on order." The old slate was still stacked out back waiting for the new.

This caused PJ to think back on something the visiting Crossroads preacher had said to make his point to the congregation. He proclaimed, "The man who has a true calling is truly fortunate."

To PJ, it seemed as likely it would be the other way around, for a person like Joe Truehaw was as blessed on one side as he was damned on the other.

The preacher had gone on to tell the story of a young man who was out of work, tempted by right and by left. He said, "One day the young man was out on the road, trying to catch a ride to a place he didn't know when he looked up and saw a message in the sky."

"Spelled out there in the clouds, clear as white chalk on

a blackboard, were the letters GPC, which he interpreted to mean, Go Preach Christ. Believing this to be a true calling that God had gone to the trouble to make so clear, he declared himself saved and set out to administer the Word."

But it turned out, according to the preacher's story, that the man was neither handy with parish nor pulpit. His congregation eventually concluded that the young man had gotten the message wrong. They had prayed on it, and together they had figured out that it was more likely that the young pastor's true calling was to Go Plow Corn.

PJ wondered how you would know if you were called. How would you know what you are called to? Was it that Joe Truehaw had misread the signs in the sky? At least, it didn't appear that he was called to plow corn.

PJ's clothes were wet and heavy. He was getting chilled.

A low growl from behind him caused him to stand up and move suddenly away. He couldn't see him but knew that Hezekiah was somewhere under the wagon. Hezekiah was old and mean-tempered, not at all the helpful hog dog that he knew Buzz to be.

"You watch out now," PJ told him. "I'm not bothering you." He had tried to make friends with this dog. There wasn't much hope for it. He reached up and took a hoe from a hook on the harness room wall. He squatted there with his back to the wall.

The dog growled again. "You're going to git a knot on your head," he said. "You just try me."

PJ leaned back against the weathered boards, the hoe resting on his knees. "Every man, every animal, every thing has its place and duty to perform," the preacher had said. And, in his heart, PJ had forgiven Hezekiah. He concluded, "He only did his duty as he knew it."

PJ had begged Joe to let the dog live. The place on the back of his leg where Hezekiah had taken a bite out of his calf was a long time healing. But, even now, PJ knew that was the way it should be.

His hand on the outside of his wet pants caressed the place where the flesh had been torn away. There was still a big punk knot there. That place felt the cold before anywhere else on his body.

He was wondering about Buzz, and how was doing, when he looked up and saw Joe standing in the entrance to the wagon shed. His hair was oiled and combed straight back. His clothes were clean and dry and he was wearing his Sunday shoes.

Joe was looking at PJ in a mischievous way, like something special that he was very proud of had happened, when Joey Lou stepped shyly out from behind him.

Joey Lou was wearing a dress.

THE FANCY MEAL

Joey Lou had driven the three of them over to the Purdee house in her pickup. PJ had gone immediately to the boys' room to change out of his wet clothes and to put on something suitable for company.

Everybody else was already seated at the table when PJ joined them in the warm but cramped kitchen. Their everyday oilcloth had already been replaced by the Sunday spread, it was the one that had the embroidery work around the edges. Their best knives, forks and spoons rested on cloth napkins, all in proper order. At every plate was a glass of sweet tea with chips of store-bought ice floating around inside. The smell in the kitchen was of bacon and cornbread, among PJ's true favorites.

He quickly sat when he saw that they all were ready to say the blessing. Belle asked Joe to say it, and he did, and PJ thought he did a good job. His mother then got up and started serving the food.

"It's raw. . . ?" PJ almost spilled his iced tea when Belle set the plate of meat on the table. ". . . . We're not going to eat this raw!" He couldn't believe what he was seeing. Belle's blood-red roast had been cut up into pieces the size of store-bought bubble gum, and nothing more. It was not cooked.

He turned in anger to Roy who sat across from him. "You're the one the cause of this."

"You cook it, dummy," Roy said.

"It's fondue, PJ." Belle put her hand on his to soothe his surprise and anger. "Here, let me show you." His mother skewered a cube of beef on her fork and stuck it into a small pot sitting on a trivet in the center of the table.

A candle was heating up the bottom of the pot. The meat sizzled, giving off the aroma of hot butter. The cooking pot was new. PJ hadn't seen anything like this before.

"It's the latest thing," Roy said. . . "It's the way we're gonna eat in style when we get over there in Florida."

"You keep out of it, Roy," Belle interrupted.

PJ was still mad. "What was Roy doing while he was supposed to be cooking this roast? Did you ask him that?"

"That's enough, PJ," Belle said quietly. "I don't want to hear any more about that. We got company, and we're not in any hurry. Let's just enjoy the fact that we are together here tonight."

Still mad, PJ turned to his mother abruptly and said out loud. "What's Roy mean when he says: 'When we get over there in Florida'"?

"PJ, I must ask you to lower your voice. After supper, I am planning on us having a talk with our friends, the Truehaws, about our future. Please be patient. . . Do you think you can do that?"

PJ took a breath and stepped back. His mother had just quit her job. That was what she was asking for, so he decided that is what he needed to do. That is what he did.

Belle was wearing white. Her blouse had two buttons open at the top. Around her neck she had fixed a small red ribbon.

She had combed her hair down so that it flared out in back and to the sides, just brushing her shoulders as she moved.

To PJ, she smelled of perfume and was giving off heat.

Belle lit candles in several places and switched off the overhead light. With her high heels on she was the tallest one in the room. "May I pour you some wine, Joe?" she asked.

"I believe I will," Joe said, raising his glass.

"Joey Lou?"

Joey Lou was squeezed in against the refrigerator. She sat stiff and erect in a kitchen chair with handmade slats and a deer hide seat. Her flour sack print dress was clean and freshly pressed. She had clipped a pink barrette in her short hair. "Yes ma'am, I'll take a little," she said.

All this dressing up seemed strange and uncomfortable to PJ. He wondered whether Joey Lou's girl things might have been from her mother. He had known Joey Lou for a long time and had never seen her wear anything closely resembling feminine paraphernalia.

"Wine, Roy?"

"Sure."

"PJ?"

"Y'all go ahead on. I'll just have some water." He heard in his own choice of words that he had used a Negro expression. He really would have wanted to try what wine tasted like, but too many changes were happening too fast already.

Belle pointed to the bowl of potatoes that PJ figured must have been cooked, since they were steaming. "Joe, why don't you start these around. Y'all can be butterin' your potatoes while we're waiting for the fondue. Here's some Kraft cheese and some crispy bacon to sprinkle on 'em, if any of you would like that. . . PJ, you can cut the cornbread."

The meal was good, PJ thought. Better than he expected. The fondue worked out all right because you could cook your meat up crisp if you wanted to, and you could put whatever you wanted to on it, like ketchup or horseradish mustard.

The potatoes were just about the best he had ever eaten, but he thought that may have been because they were eating so late and he was really hungry. That there was plenty of food and drink to go around pleased him. That is the way it should be, when neighbors come to visit. He actually couldn't remember when they had ever had a sit-down dinner with company.

After supper, PJ rinsed the plates and Joey Lou dried them. He had lit the coal oil lamp and put it on the edge of the sink because Belle wouldn't let them turn on the electric light, which was a single bulb hanging down from the ceiling on a cord. Belle and Joe just stayed at the table to share a cigarette.

Wisps of cigarette smoke were soon escaping from the kitchen and made their way along the ceiling of the living room. Over by the window in the living room, Roy cleared everything off the small end table, including the radio and several of their

Marvel comics, and positioned the record player on it.

Roy then went out and brought in the whole box of records he had been keeping in the two boys' bedroom since he had taken an interest in getting to know Itchy Gates better.

The record album box was a wooden crate with a picture of grapes on it that read "California Raisins." The records were divided by those that were 78s and 33s and 45s, each still in the sleeves of their original labels, all standing up in neat even rows.

Belle was telling Joe, "When it's the end of the week and payday at the plant, the people at the Five and Dime have come to expect to see me heading for the music aisle. Just when I walk in the door, they automatically announce, 'Belle's here.' And the first thing I say is, 'What you got new from the Hit Parade?' And they tell me, 'Belle, you've got to be our very best customer for records.'"

Roy had climbed up on a chair and plugged their portable Victrola into an extension cord coming from the ceiling light. "Every one of these records she's listened to a hundred times," he said aloud. "The old ones, she's listened to two hundred times."

"I have," Belle spoke up in agreement from the kitchen. "At least that."

Roy added, as he climbed down, "This record player often runs way into the night. Sometimes it's goin' and she's sound asleep."

"With that many records," Joe Truehaw added, "You could start your own radio station."

"They add up," Belle agreed as she went over and chose a record from the box. She took it out of the sleeve and held it against her breast.

When Roy was ready, he reached and took the disc from her, being careful not to touch anything except the edge. He blew on it to remove any possible lint or dust, and gently positioned it on the turntable. He moved the arm into position over the record very slowly and carefully, so the tune would start at the right place and at the right moment.

Before he had heard more than a second's worth of sound, PJ recognized what record it was. It was a piece from the Glenn Miller orchestra. He knew it immediately because it was a game they used to play as a family.

Two of them would close their eyes and the other would take out a record and set the needle down on the first groove of the disc or in the middle or anywhere, and the game was to see who could identify that musical piece the fastest.

Belle nearly always won. PJ could get it too, but it took him longer. Roy was also very fast at this kind of thing.

Except for the music and the cigarette smoke that traveled along the ceiling, everything in the room stopped. Nobody moved. Nobody said anything. They just listened, and breathed quietly in and out, as if journeying to fantastic and unimaginable places.

From an unpainted tenant house on the rural Sandy Prairie the Trueshaws and Purdees were transported to big city ballrooms in Chicago and New York and Los Angeles.

But for PJ it was something more than that. He was aware of the gentle rain as it fell on the tin roof of their house tonight, and listening caused him to catch his breath. The smoke from Joe and Belle's cigarettes was lingering in the rafters of the ceiling, and the light from the candles and the flames of the butane stove seemed to be swimming in their home space. It was like the gentle waving of sycamore leaves catching a sudden breeze.

All of these converged, playing in perfect time with the sounds of the Glenn Miller orchestra, whose players in black tuxedos seemed half in the kitchen and half in the sitting room. Their brass instruments caught the light and their playing transformed the room.

Belle put her hand on Joe's arm. "You want to dance?"

Joe was leaning back in his chair, studying the canning jars on top of the refrigerator. When he felt her touch, he was momentarily startled. "I don't hardly remember how," he said, as if to be honest.

"Sure you do. We used to dance."

"That's right," he agreed.

They stood. Belle kicked off her shoes and gave him her hand. There was almost enough room for another person to stand between the two of them. At first, they didn't move. But Glenn Miller wasn't waiting. The musicians were playing.

Soon Joe's head started going up and down, and his shoulders and arms started rocking a little bit. Then his left foot moved and his right foot, and he was pushing and she was following. They went as far as the heater and turned and came back to the edge of the table.

When they started, Joe was standing as straight as a lot post, and was counting under his breath 1-2-3, 1-2-3, 1-2-3. Then, the rhythm of it seemed to clear out a space for the two of them moving together in the room.

Belle was now leaning back, her eyes closed. Her long brown hair fell past her shoulders. It moved maybe a half-second after she did, sort of staying there with a life of its own, like her hair was having a hard time keeping up.

"I can't remember when I last danced," she said. She drew Joe closer to her and put her head on his shoulder.

Joe looked like he was holding a bucket of sweet milk to his chest and was praying it wouldn't spill.

The record ended. Joe and Belle separated. Joe shook himself as if his muscles were tense from being under such strain. "You're an awfully good dancer," he said. "I like it."

"Come on, boys," Belle said. "Let's you dance too."

"We could play dominoes?" PJ offered as an alternative.

"I've never danced," Joey Lou admitted. "Not once. I wouldn't know the first thing about it."

"It's easy once you catch on to it. Roy and me will show you." Belle motioned to Roy, who came over and took his mother's hand. It looked like Roy wasn't at all scared of it. At first Belle was leading, but soon Roy was leading her. "Like that," Belle said. "Joe . . . you show her."

Standing erect, Joe Truehaw took his daughter in his arms, adjusted their position and made a move forward. It didn't work. Their legs got entangled and the two of them almost fell over.

"Let me try with Joey Lou," Belle said. The others stood and watched. It seemed Joey Lou was more confident when Belle was her partner. When she could lead, she got the rhythm of it.

"Now Roy and Joey Lou?" Belle directed.

Roy was cocky and overly sure of himself. He took Joey Lou's right hand in his left and put his right hand on her waist. But something was missing. He reached around and helped her put her left hand on his shoulder. They waited a moment listening for the beat of the music. He tried to push forward but she wasn't budging.

"It doesn't feel right," Joey Lou complained. She took his hand from her waist and put her hand on his waist. "This feels better." Starting with the beat, she tried to push him but he wouldn't move.

"That's wrong," Roy said. He reversed the position of their hands. She took them away. He put both his hands on her waist and her hands on his shoulder and tried to move her, without success.

"I don't know why he has to lead," Joey Lou complained to the others. She took both his hands and put them on her shoulders, and she pushed. That didn't work either.

Joe spoke up, trying to be helpful, "Go along with it, Honey. It's just the way it's done. The man leads."

In quick reply, she said, "I wouldn't trust Roy Purdee to lead me to the door of the outhouse."

."Come here, PJ" Joey Lou said. "I'm goin' to see if you can do this. Roy's too stubborn."

"I'm not sure I can do it either," PJ told her.

"We're goin' to see."

PJ had been the victim of Joey Lou's arm wrestling holds, which he had survived, so he decided to trust her.

She took the dominant position and waited for the music to begin. PJ was up on his toes trying not to get stepped on. Joey Lou was strong and determined. He began to catch on and keep up. They moved. Yes, they began to actually dance around the kitchen using the exaggerated steps of a waltz.

PJ was amazed that they could do that, and do it to the music. He felt pleased and proud of himself and especially for Joey Lou.

They were dancing in exact rhythm with the other.

Joe and Belle both applauded and told them how well they did.

Roy and their mother then got up to dance in the same space. Roy was leading and also doing well, but they were soon bumping into Joey Lou and PJ.

"Watch out where you are going," PJ said in self-defense. He could have predicted this would happen. That was just Roy joking around, being aggravating and disruptive for no good reason.

Joey Lou took the challenge and started aiming PJ in the direction of Roy and his mom, like they did with bumper cars at the fair.

Roy warned, "You better control that bus."

Joey Lou started acting silly, reaching all the way around PJ and tickling him under the arm because he was so serious.

Trying to keep a straight face, PJ protested, "I'm not ticklish."

To the others, Joey Lou reported, "PJ says he's not goosey, so he won't mind if I just run my fingers up here." And she tickled him some more.

It was all meant to be fun, but it was more than PJ could take, so he broke free and went over and turned the Victrola down low. When he found the right record to calm everything down, he put it on.

Standing and addressing the room, he said directly to his mother and to Roy, using his hard-earned 14-year-old voice, "Now I want my family to tell me what this Florida thing is all about."

There was a long pause before Belle got up and went into the kitchen. She returned with an envelope in her hand. PJ wondered if it was the same envelope she had taken from the mailbox when they came home in the rain from the store.

"PJ, please sit down," his mother directed. He went and sat by Joey Lou. Belle was the only one who remained standing. "Before I read you this letter, there are some things I need to tell you all."

Belle was clearly near tears as she spoke. "My father, Jim

Carr, has been in touch with Grandee Purdee about some kind of reconciliation with our family."

There was a long pause in which no one spoke. "Actually, it wasn't my father. It was his new wife, Ina Mae, who called Grandee on the telephone, and talked to her several times. Gran told me that Miss Ina Mae said my father felt really bad about what happened, but didn't know how to make it right between us."

Belle took a deep breath. "And I guess I am as prideful as anybody in not being willing to forgive him for what he did." Tears were coming to her eyes.

She then straighted up and read the contents of the letter she held in her hand. It was from Ina Mae Carr, addressed:

Jim and Ina Mae Carr
1100 North West Terrace, Mason Manor Estates
Gainesville, Florida

Belle,

You and I have never met and I expect that you know absolutely nothing about me. But your father and I want to correct that.

First of all, he acknowledges what he did was a mistake. Being estranged from his daughter and not getting to know his two grandsons has weighed on him. He now agrees with me that we need to try to put all that behind us, and we should live in the future as a family.

Maybe it is too late, but he and I want us to give it a try getting to know each other and see if we can learn how to heal this broken relationship.

As you may know, we have recently moved to Gainesville, where Jim is now the basketball coach at the University. The Christmas season is approaching. We have a big house with plenty of room. Since we hardly know anybody here, we would like to invite you and the boys to come for Christmas, and stay a week or two if you are willing.

If you want to write, use the above address. Our long-distance telephone number is 374-3602 Gainesville. Yes, it is a private line.

Jim and I have talked and we are in agreement on this. Enclosed is a check for $100 that Jim and I hope you will use to get here.

Ina Mae Carr

Dec. 27, 1950

Dear Grandee

We are in Florida! Roy and I sent you some postcards on our way out here. We hope you got them.

The generator went out on our car somewhere past Biloxi. We ended up sleeping on the beach. I've never done anything like that. It was cold but worth it. A fellow in a big pickup helped jump-start us next morning. We found a junkyard where Roy and I bought an almost new battery, and they loaned us some tools. We really didn't lose much time.

We got to Gainesville the day before Christmas. When we found where the University was, we knew the Carrs didn't live very far away.

You can write us at 11 Northwest Terrace, Gainesville, Florida. This is where Belle's parents live. They are really nice people. At first, Roy and me were having a hard time calling them Grandma and Grandpa. They told us to just call them Coach Carr and Miss Ina Mae, so that is what we are doing.

P.S. If you see Lee Junior, please tell him we got here, and that my next letter is going to be to him.

Your loving grandson

PJ

Dec. 28, 1950

Dear Lee Junior:

I hope Grandee shared my letter to her with you. Roy and me are living high off the hog here in Florida.

Everybody around here will be sure to know that it is Christmas because all the stores, churches and even houses are decorated with colored lights, and some of them blink on and off. Some are just left on all night long.

Our new grandparents, Coach Jim Carr and his wife Ina Mae, live in a neighborhood where all the streets are made of poured concrete. They have sidewalks leading to almost anywhere you want to go.

The Carr house is so big that there is a special room for viewing television and another one for getting exercise. Belle, Roy and I each have separate rooms, each with its own bathroom.

Tell Poppy I appreciate the SHOOTER he made for me as a going-away present. Would you give him this drawing I made? He can hang it in his room if he likes. I don't yet know where the creeks and ponds are around here, but I can't wait to go out with my backpack and plunk some turtles.

Say hello to Nettie, to Glory and the rest of the Johnson family.

You write, you hear?

Your best friend

PJ

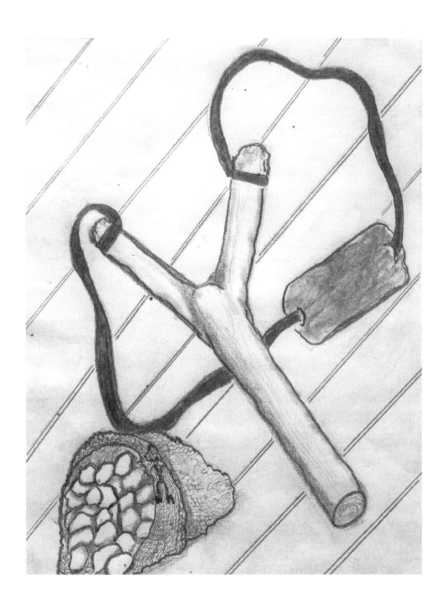

January 8, 1951

Dear Grandee,

I don't know whether Belle wrote you, but I thought I ought to send you a short note to let you know what is going on here.

Our new Grandmother and Grandfather are take-charge people. With their help, Belle has just interviewed for a job as a receptionist in a dentist office here in Gainesville.

I am afraid to tell you, if she gets it, we will have to stay here. Roy and me will be going to a school that is bigger than the whole Theodosa County fairgrounds, and Belle will be wearing high heels and dresses to work.

Yesterday, she and Miss Ina Mae went to the after-Christmas sales at a local Shopping Center. And they gave the rest of us a fashion show when they got back.

I think our Mom is really liking this go-to-town stuff. But the thing she seems to be enjoying most is sleeping in on Saturdays and Sundays.

P.S. I love you. And I miss you very much.

Your Grandson

PG

January 26, 1951

Dear Lee Junior,

It looks like we are going to stay in Florida, for a while anyway. Belle just got a job.

Our Mom is now a receptionist in an office for dentists. Can you believe they have air conditioning, even in the winter, and none of these offices are open on Saturdays? How about that!

Roy and I go to the same school now. We ride the same bus, but we don't see each other because he is over at the High School, and I am in what is called Middle School.

About 100 people live in the two-story apartment building we just moved into. I came to that number by counting the mailboxes out front. We live on the second floor, but there is an elevator you can ride if you don' want to walk.

Our new apartment came with plates and cups and pots and pans and forks and knives— almost anything you need! It has a gas stove, an electric refrigerator and a dining table with matching chairs.

In the kitchen, there is a telephone we can use to call local or long-distance. Out back there is a swimming pool (made of concrete) and a bunch of tennis courts that we can sign-up for, but they are free. You do have to bring your own racquet and ball.

I will tell you straight. I miss the Prairie and everybody that I know there.

I feel bad that I won't be there to help you Johnsons with your new truck farming operation.

Most of all, I will miss working at the cotton gin once it starts up again.
Please tell Mr. Sapp what I said!

P.S: Belle promised Roy and me that in the spring sometime we will be able to come back to get our things and say goodbye to everybody. Right now, we are not sure when that will be.

Your best friend

Pg

March 4, 1951

Dear Lee Junior:

Hallelujah! Belle says we can set the date.
We will be coming back to visit during our
Spring Break: March 16 to March 23.

By driving all night, we should get there by
late Saturday. Grandee is insisting we stay with
her, so we will be sleeping up at the Big House.
I can't wait.

Do you want to come climb up in the attic
with me to see if there are any hanging chicken
snakes still up there?

I have been doing some new drawings, I
wanted you and your family to have these
to keep. One is a drawing I did of the old
cemetery. The details may not be perfect since
I drew it from memory. I still cannot get it
out of my mind that hardly anybody knows or
cares what happened to the SAMBO people after
they were shipped here to America. I want Mr.
Dunfee and all your family to know that I do
care.

Maybe at the next Juneteenth celebration you
can share this picture with Rev. Lovsee Light,
and he can tell that story again, even if the
families can no longer get to where the graves
are.

The other drawing is a greatly enlarged copy
from a U.S. War Department photo that I found
in the things Belle was going to throw away. It
is a picture of the Navy trainer my father was
flying when he dive-bombed the Sandy Prairie

School. His love letter to Belle was folded up in a cartridge attached to a yellow silk parachute, which I now have.

Your Friend always

PJ

March 6, 1951

Dear Lee Junior:

The post office sold me this box for 15 cents. I asked for something big enough to hold all of these envelopes. I am wanting to hear from people, so I thought they would more likely write if I addressed and put stamps on a bunch of these.

Would you give these out, please?

I also include some of my old pencil sketches. You can show these around, but I was thinking that you and the rest of the Johnson family might want to tack them up somewhere in the house.

Today, I finished a drawing that I did just for you. It is a picture of the house our new grandparents live in here in Gainesville. This is where we stayed over Christmas when we first got to Florida. Pretty fancy house, wouldn't you say?

Do you see the basketball hoop in the front yard? I must tell you that Coach Carr has been showing Roy and me how to do lay-ups, jump shots and free throws. We aren't that good, but we are getting better. And he is really a nice guy.

Your best friend,

PJ